Edward William Lewis Davies

Dartmoor Days

Scenes in the Forest

Edward William Lewis Davies

Dartmoor Days
Scenes in the Forest

ISBN/EAN: 9783337397777

Printed in Europe, USA, Canada, Australia, Japan

Cover: Foto ©Andreas Hilbeck / pixelio.de

More available books at **www.hansebooks.com**

DARTMOOR DAYS

OR

SCENES IN THE FOREST.

A POEM.

BY THE

REV. E. W. L. DAVIES, M.A.

'Flumina amem sylvasque inglorius.'

LONDON:
LONGMAN, GREEN, LONGMAN, ROBERTS, & GREEN.
1863.

TO

HIS ROYAL HIGHNESS

THE PRINCE OF WALES

AND

DUKE OF CORNWALL

ETC.

THIS POEM IS

BY GRACIOUS PERMISSION

MOST HUMBLY DEDICATED

BY

HIS ROYAL HIGHNESS'S

FAITHFUL AND MOST OBEDIENT SERVANT,

THE AUTHOR.

ARGUMENT.

HE scene of the following poem is laid chiefly within the Forest of Dartmoor. In the first part, the time of action includes a week in the month of November; in the second, a week in May. The *dramatis personæ* are a party of gentlemen more or less connected with the County of Devon.

DARTMOOR DAYS.

PART FIRST.

I

COME, Goddess of the silver bow,

Forth to the woodlands let us go ;

Oh come with him who loves to own

The glories of thy sylvan throne ;

Who, from his youth, has bowed the knee

In wild ecstatic love for thee ;

And ever from that day has been

Devoted to his forest Queen.

Oft has he viewed thy maiden grace

In every form that marks the chase ;

B

And often on the flood and fell,

Pursued the charms he loved so well:

Then aid him as he takes to wing

And woodland joys attempts to sing.

II

Far in Devonia's favoured land

Extends a forest wild and grand;

Where oozing forth with gentle song

Trickles the tiny Dart along;

But ere it quits the peaty soil

The infant waters chafe and boil,

And, rushing on with mighty roar,

Awake the woods from shore to shore.

Here fountains that perennial seem

The source of many a noble stream,

Rise sparkling from the Giver's hands
And wend their way to grateful lands:
They charm the eye where'er they flow,
They bless the verdant meads below,
And bear upon their bosom-tide
A world of commerce far and wide.

III

Yet higher far than fountains rise,
The giant tors approach the skies;
And often on their rugged breast
The slumbering clouds are seen to rest;
Jove was a better judge, I trow,
In days of old than he is now;
When Juno on her bosom fair
Sustained Ixion's form in air.

With boulder upon boulder piled
The frowning structures crown the wild;
Thus Ossa upon Pelion nods,
The work of men at war with gods.
At eve to strangers they would seem
Like castles of a troubled dream,
Or play-work of some giant race
Who pitched and tossed them into place—
Those pillars that support the sky
Were landmarks of a world gone by:
Long ere the ark was under weigh
Yon granite tors were old and grey:
Untouched by time or other foes,
They mocked the deluge as it rose;
And there defiant still they stand
The pyramids of Nature's hand.

IV

And oft on highest crag is seen
An oak in miniature, I ween;
A come-by-chance, dropped from the store
Of some lone bird in passing o'er;
Rough cradle for the infant tree
Thus nurtured in adversity—
Of stunted and fantastic form,
It laughs at hurricane and storm,
And braves securely every shock,
A British oak from stem to stock—
Again, long tufts of moss depend
Fast clinging to their sturdy friend,
And waving sadly in the wind
Recall funereal plumes to mind;
Or, moistened by the misty shower
Like banner on some shattered tower,

That droops and sighs and seems to weep
The downfall of the feudal keep.

v

Majestic still the tors remain
The monarchs of the lonely plain;
And as the shades of night draw near,
They scare the peasant's soul with fear;
While thoughtful minds in them behold
The relics of the days of old,
And peering through the hazy past
Catch glimpses of the light at last.
Here Murchison may fitly trace
The records of primæval race;
And wisely from the mystic page
Draw moral for the present age:
Or Owen with ingenious brain
The secrets of the past explain.

VI

From these strongholds mayhap of yore

The Mastodon has ranged the moor,

And gamboled in the granite halls,

Or stood a siege within the walls;

While posted on the topmost stone

A Dodo held the watch alone.

Or had the region classic been,

A troop of Centaurs might be seen

Careering o'er the boundless plain,

Pursued by Lapithæ again.

Nations have come and gone since then,

And earth has changed her race of men;

Druids and Celts have passed away,

The Priests and Pagans of the day;

And misty curtains intervene

Betwixt the past and present scene;

Nor living hand is left to trace

That dim and parenthetic space.

VII

Great Mistor near the centre stands,

Looming above the dreary lands;

Here heathery wastes, and there the mires,

Surround for miles the rocky spires;

O'er hill and dale and wavy plain

The eye will seek for bounds in vain :

On every side it seems to be

Illimitable, wild, and free.

Full many a league of moss and moor

The fleetest foot may wander o'er;

But ere the farthest point it gain

The tired foot will halt with pain :

The eye may sweep the plain aright,
Still distant plains evade the sight,
And ere the wide expanse it see
The keenest eye will weary be.

VIII

Old Nature's impress marks the moor
From Heytor to the western shore ;
Shaggy and stern and unreclaimed,
She could not, if she would, be tamed.
No signs of graceful art abound
At variance with the scene around :
But barren heath and granite grey
Acknowledge Nature's potent sway ;
Her rugged features still as grand
As fashioned by the Maker's hand.

Here Solitude and Silence reign

Sole tenants of the dreary plain;

And, save the merry mountain rill,

The waste around is sad and still:

Impressive scenes that well impart

A thoughtful sense to every heart;

And to the pensive soul recall

A type of endless rest to all.

IX

Than fair Dart-meet full well I ween,

A sweeter spot was never seen:

From Cranmere's fount the waters flow

In parted streams to vales below,

And wandering here the happy twain

Like loving sisters meet again.

Beyond the hanging woods a glimpse

Tells you at once the place is Brimpts;

A hall of no pretence or fame

Save to a few who love its name;

The few who never can forget

The meetings of that joyous set,

Who years ago resorted there,

When sorrow was as light as air.

In autumn and in spring the same,

Like birds of passage there they came;

Attracted by the forest chase,

The hunting runs and killing pace;

And youthful, strong, and full of hope

They swept the plain or mountain slope.

A simple joy to cheer the mind;

A charm without a pang behind!

Ay, time itself can scarce efface

The golden light that gilds the place.

x

Forth to the battle-field they come,

Like soldiers at the beat of drum ;

Two brothers loving all that's good,

Whether in city, field or flood,

Leave, to enjoy the moorland wind,

The sunny bank of Exe behind.

The Exe may flow with silvery sands

And fertilise its fairy lands ;

Pactolus with its golden stream

May realise the poet's dream ;

With rugged Dart they can't compare,

So turbulent and yet so fair :—

Thus felt the twain when first they tried

The freedom of the mountain side ;

And evermore they'll tell with praise

Of forest meets and Dartmoor days.

XI

Another pair impart, I ween,

Fast colours to the flying scene :

Two sons of Mars, preferring far

Diana's charms to toils of war,

Have changed awhile their heavy guns

For Manton and the moorland runs.

Gallant and prompt to none they yield

Precedence on the battle field ;

And well they hold at board or chase

A social and a foremost place.

Sprung from a sire of wondrous might,

An athlete in a moral fight ;

One who for truth would calmly brave

The trials of a martyr's grave ;

Who stands on guard for Church and
   State,
A lion at the entrance gate.
On points of faith or wavering doubt
Slight menace brings the Champion out;
And woe betide the sceptic foe
That dares to meet his crushing blow.
The impress of a manly sire,
Thus early stamped, will ne'er expire;
Whether in peace or war it be,
The fruit will bless the parent tree.

XII

Ah! Postumé, it makes me sigh
To ponder on the years gone by;
The sun obscured by many a cloud,
The wintry winds so long and loud;

Life's crosses and their future ends,

But most of all the loss of friends :—

In mercy were they sent we know,

To wean us from a world of woe.

Full twenty years have passed away

And left us shaken, sere and grey,

Since joyous we foregathered there

The pastime of the field to share—

Ah ! well I mind the gladsome morn,

When Strongshield with his hounds and
  horn

At six o'clock announced it day,

And forth to Cator bent his way.

XIII

Stout were his hounds and fleet his steed,

He valued them for bone and breed;

And rarely failed the day to crown

By hunting till the sun went down—

Brave Figaro and foxhound blood

Were suited to his ardent mood,

And in the chase full well he knew

His horse was staunch, his hounds were

    true.

The sport ambitious riders spoil

Would cause his Norman blood to boil;

And oft upon the grassy plain

He rated them with just disdain;

But elements so soon disturbed

Were lulled to rest by one soft word;

As vapours fly before the wind

And leave a cloudless sky behind.

But deep you need to probe the man

The virtues of his heart to scan,

And scarce you'd find a truer friend

From Berwick to the far Land's End.

XIV

   This day o'er Cator-down they go

As straight as ever flew a crow;

Bashful and Buxom strive in vain

A lead upon the pack to gain ;

The hounds ahead, the men apart,

Are plunging through the angry Dart ;

Up Lartor hill away they sweep,

Like swallows o'er the placid deep :

No work for Harry's whip to-day,

The Hermit wants it more than they.

The bursting pace and heavy land

Have brought the Hermit to a stand ;

C

And spite of beans and Harry's luck*

The gallant steed is fairly stuck,

A fixture in a lonely spot,

Well suited to a Hermit's lot.

XV

With heartfelt sorrow Vesey sees

The Dwarf is going ill at ease:

Oft had he proved him tough and strong,

No work too fast, no day too long;

And now his sob and panting state

Proclaim aloud his coming fate;

But Vesey for his beast can feel,

And spares alike the whip and steel;

* Our friend Harry had brought a bag of beans with him for the use of his two horses; but his groom, on the *à fortiori* principle, administered them so liberally, that he succeeded not in giving vigour and endurance to his hunters, but in damaging the eyes of at least one of them.

With steady hand he strives to guide

His rolling gait and heavy stride;

But all in vain : broad meanings tell

The little horse has gone too well.

The Gunner on his chestnut steed

The flying squadron tries to lead;

He keeps one eye on leading hound,

The other on the boggy ground :

On harder soil he makes his play

And collars Fitz upon the grey;

But still his tactics will not do,

The chestnut horse has cast a shoe;

And, though defeat is hard to bear,

He yields to fate and drops to rear;

Then limbers up and quits the van,

'A sadder and a wiser man.'

XVI

Meanwhile the pack is dashing on :
Yonder they go ; and now they 're gone ;
The moorman for his winter fire
Is stacking turf in Lartor mire,
And past him as they seem to fly
He longs for wings to join the cry ;
For well he knows the pace they go,
No human foot could travel so ;
So cheering them with might and main
He settles to his work again.
O'er Bellivor they race along,
No music from the tuneful throng ;
Till checking at the tor they found
The sinking game had gone to ground.

Thus brutes and mortals fare the same,

The baffled hounds will miss their game,

And man will fail the prize to clasp

Just as it seems within his grasp.

XVII

But wearied steeds and hounds and men

Are safely mustered once again :

A few pale stars affect to shine

And light us on our homeward line.

The woodcock now upon the wing

Is flitting past to upland spring ;

The fern-owl wheels above the brake,

The heron screams from yonder lake ;

The Dart is moaning down the dell

Like music from a muffled bell :

Brimpts is at hand ! we quit the field,

And then the doom of day is sealed.

The products of the farm afford

A homely and a welcome board ;

The stirring chase and mountain air

Give relish to a simple fare. *

No dishes wrought with Gallic skill

The gastronomic rites fulfill ;

No French device imparts a cheer,

Nor King of Oude is wanted here :

The native art is all we need

For mutton of the Dartmoor breed :

Dame Coaker's eye has watched the spit,

And Rab has helped to baste a bit ;

---

* 'Jejunus raró stomachus vulgaria temnit.'—*Hor.*

'Go work, hunt, exercise ! (he thus began)
Then scorn a homely dinner if you can.'—*Pope.*

And French would make the dinner out
With Hornywinks instead of trout.*

XVIII

The hearty meal is scarcely made,
And benediction duly said,
Ere casting back we glibly trace
The features of the morning chase ;
And every acre of the plain
Is hunted on the board again.
A lofty pile of well-dried peat
Imparts a strong and genial heat ;
And tales of sport that never tire
Are told around the glowing fire ;
While goblets filled with mountain dew
Invigorate the frame anew.

* Hornywink is the Dartmoor name for the peewit.

Come Fitz, my boy, that ballad sing,

A charming stave ; pray do begin ;

We all implore : and soft and clear

' The Four-leaved shamrock' greets the ear :

He tells a tale of magic weal,

The sorrows of the heart to heal,

That he who finds the fairy leaf

May charm away the mourner's grief.

XIX

Then Strongshield, who delights in song,

Applauds the minstrel loud and long ;

And well he wraps his hearty praise

In lively thought and pleasant phrase :

Nor fails to add how well the grey

Had carried Fitz throughout the day ;

That Figaro he hoped to find
Had dropped the grey a mile behind ;
But close to hounds he rode astern,
And Fitz was there at every turn.
Then Strongshield with an air of fun
Straight at the Gunner points a gun ;
He tells him 't is by all agreed
That want of powder stopped his steed :
A case of hors-de-combat true,
He lost his wind and *then* his shoe.
But why is Vesey so engrossed,
Unmindful of the passing toast ;
And why so pensively he twirls
The lock that on his forehead curls ?
Mayhap he now recalls with pain
The struggles of the Dwarf again ;
Or deeply he deplores the need
Of fire and physic for the steed !

Ah no ! he keeps the secret close,

Far other thoughts his soul engross :

That shamrock song has brought to mind

A syren voice he left behind.

But now to rest : the time is ten ;

To-morrow to the field again.

XX

November's gloom is felt aright

When every star is veiled by night,

And darkness, undisturbed by sound,

Hovers on solemn wings around.

Such night it was : the desert gloom

Was dark and silent as the tomb ;

The hanging clouds had ceased to weep,

And Dart herself was hushed to sleep.

Scarce do the hunters rise to quit

The board of social mirth and wit ;

The kind 'good night' is on the tongue,

The friendly hand is scarcely wrung,

When distant shouts their steps arrest,

And baulk them of the promised rest.

But what the sounds or whence they rise

Creates at once intense surprise ;

No ghostly cause the hunters sought—

They never gave it once a thought ;

But calling for their cudgels stout,

They grasped them and they sallied out.

What eye can pierce the Stygian shade

Which night upon the earth has laid ?

Sharp ears alone must serve to guide

Their footsteps to the river side ;

For well, I trow, in forest land

Those shouts proceed from lawless band,

Exulting o'er their gasping prey,

Like demons keeping holiday.

XXI

Soon they approach the frowning wood

That overhangs the eastern flood ;

Watchful and mute, in Indian file,

They move ahead or pause awhile.

Avoiding now the shaft of tin

Where gallant Gliscar toppled in ;

They wind around the rocky ledge,

And safely gain the river's edge.

With sudden glare a blazing light

Bursts on the hunters' dazzled sight ;

In rough mid-stream, on boulder stone,

A stalwart peasant stands alone ;

Aloft, on granite rock so grey,

The savage bears despotic sway ;

Fierce are the words of his command,

And bright the torch he holds in hand.

Casting a wild, unearthly gleam,

That dances o'er the rapid stream.

Transparent now the waters flow,

Revealing things of life below ;

The troutlets in the crystal tide

Their beauty-spots are fain to hide,

And salmon, as they see the ray,

Mistake it for the beam of day.

XXII

Another, on a boulder near,

Is poising high a deadly spear ;

On pedestal erect he trod,

The model of a river God.

Fixed and intent, with heron eye,

A fish at work he seems to spy ;

Too near, alas! to that fell hand

A salmon ploughs the gravel sand ;

In furrow deep beneath the wave

Her tender young she hopes to save ;

Imbedded with a mother's care,

The seed is sown and fostered there.

Little the savage recks, I trow,

Of thousands slain by single blow ;

As little does he deem it sin

To kill a fish so lank and thin ;

The sanctity of Nature's law

He values as a worthless straw.

XXIII

The torchlight, as a solar ray,

Attracts the unsuspecting prey ;

And now the shaft is raised with skill,

Obedient to the ruffian's will ;

That brawny arm a minute more

Had hurled the gasping fish ashore ;

But, as the hunters hurried on,

With sudden splash the light is gone ;

And though they seized the lifted spear,

They failed to clutch the mountaineer.

Reckless, he plunged adown the wave,

As though he sought an instant grave ;

But love of life was strong in him,

And, practised well to dive or swim,

He battled with the flood amain,

And quickly reached the shore again.

Poor Palinuxus, when he fell,

Went headlong to the gates of hell ;

But here the poacher's lighter fate

Was ended by a prison gate :

And often has he told the tale,

Carousing o'er his stoup of ale,

How fearlessly in hasty flight

He swam the Dart at dead of night;

And how he hoped to see the day,

In winter month as well as May,

When every man might take his spear

And kill a salmon round the year.

XXIV

The remnant of the poacher crew

Like phantoms to the forest flew ;

Ah ! little then his comrades cared

How ill the luckless spearman fared ;

Safety in flight alone they find,

The gloom ahead, the foe behind.

A pair of salmon, long and black,

Are captured on the felon's track :

Alas! unfit for human food,

They slay the fish and rob the flood:

Nor so unwise were they of old

Who killed the goose to gain the gold.

That noble Dart, Devonia's pride,

Might feed and cheer the country-side;

The swift prolific stream should yield

Its treasures like a fertile field.

As Egypt's mighty waters rise,

What boundless wealth the Nile supplies!

Her gentle bosom heaves to give

The food on which her children live;

Needless the aid of rain or dew

To stimulate the soil anew;

But spreading fatness o'er the land

She blesses man with copious hand,

D

And arms him with the staff of life—

The sickle—for the sword of strife.

Again, where Great Columbia flows,

Nor want nor care the Indian knows;

The rolling flood is made to pay

Its tribute ere it rolls away :

The prowling race with rare device

The salmon to their traps entice ;

And summer stock or winter hoard

With ample measure crowns their board.

XXV

In England too in olden times

Productive were her crystal mines ;

When every streamlet had its store

Of boundless wealth in living ore ;

And salmon in the mountain burn

Came cropping out at every turn.

At little cost the homely poor

Found plenty at their very door,

And raised their grateful voice to Heaven

In token of the blessing given.

In early spring fresh-run from sea,

King of the finny world was he ;

And still he reigned in summer tide

The angler's joy, the river's pride.

XXVI

But when brown autumn shed her store

And summer sun was felt no more ;

When whirled about by every wind

No rest the withered leaf could find ;

When angry floods outstepped their beds,

And salmon leaped the river-heads;

Then wisely by the law 't was found

That spawning beds were sacred ground;

Swift, brawling streams and shallows fair

Were guarded with a jealous care;

And Vulture he was deemed for aye

Who made a spawning fish his prey.

If civic knights for once could share

The food of gods, ambrosial fare;

With envy would Olympus quake

To hear the praise of salmon-flake:

That creamy, firm, nutritious food

That renovates the human blood,

And makes fastidious mortals own

It stands unrivalled and alone.

A RED SKY.

When rosy-fingered morn appears,

Her smile of joy will melt to tears,

And early hunters ne'er forget

That ruddy skies betoken wet.

As chanticleer had hailed the morn

Up-roused by Strongshield's cheery horn;

Both Harry and the Celt obey

The summons at the break of day.

But Fitz and Vesey, still in lair,

Hear the reveille with despair,

And claim a trifle more of rest,

To get themselves and horses dressed.

No laggards they; but ever true,

They see a distant lurid hue

O'er Yartor spread: and well they say,

'No hunting on the moor to-day.'

XXVIII

Not tempest of an eastern plain

That strikes to earth the pilgrim train,

When clouds of sand are whirling by

That parch the tongue and fire the eye :

Not fogs that hide the rock-bound shore

From ship at sea, are dreaded more

Than those dark mists of fatal gloom

That make the moor a living tomb.

The hunter homeward speeds in haste,

Ere fogs o'ertake him on the waste ;

And if to Foxtor mires he roam,

He'll bid a long adieu to home ;

A dreary shroud is o'er his head,

A yawning swamp around him spread ;

Spell-bound and lost he ventures on

One fatal step—and all is done ;

Hopeless his struggles, vain his throes,

Deeper and deeper down he goes !

The raven claps her ebon wing,

His dirge the howling winds may sing,

And mists will spread the last sad pall

O'er that dark grave unknown to all.

XXIX

To solve the many doubts that rise,

Tom French is called to judge the skies.

The stork discerning clime from clime,

Observes his own appointed time ;

The swallow and the turtle-dove

Derive their instinct from above ;

And Tom's perception clear and strong,

When tested thus, was rarely wrong.

He saw and thought the lurid morn

Was adverse to the hound and horn :

' I knew,' he said, ' it would be so,

' And fed the hounds an hour ago ;

' The Dart ne'er cries from Holne in vain,

' But gets her fill of fog or rain :

' *I reckon 't would be bad to try*

' *Your honour know'th so well as I.*'

No shepherd of the Grampian range

Ere marked an atmospheric change

With keener eye ; from youth to age

He loved and studied Nature's page ;

And she to cherish love so true

Had taught her pupil all he knew.

XXX

Tom's glint of eye was such, I ween,
As in a fox alone is seen ;
Astute and clear, it seemed to claim
The vigour of a double brain ;
The instinct of the brute combined
With reason of the human mind.
Withal 't was marvellous to see
His ready turn for repartee ;
He ne'er was challenged, but he 'd hit
With apt reply and native wit.
With foxes Tom, in early life,
Had waged for years a deadly strife ;
He murdered them no matter how,
And shot them as he 'd shoot a crow.

Backed by a leash of half-bred hounds
And terriers ever scarred with wounds;
This ragged crew gave little grace
Or quarter to the vulpine race.

XXXI

The line of every prowling fox
From Goodamoor to Heytor rocks,
The otter holts on Dart or Plym,
Though hid from sight, were known to him.
He drove the pregnant fox to earth,
And killed the vixen giving birth :
' The varmint should be killed,' he 'd say,
' On Sunday as on other day ; '
But such dark deeds, 't is very clear,
Tom has renounced for many a year,

Or Tom himself would not be nigh
Our trusty guide and true ally.

XXXII

A rolling grey and dismal fog,
Joint offspring of the cloud and bog,
Enshrouds the moor ; and all the earth
Seems boggy from its very birth.
A team of merry spaniels then
Loving the brake as well as fen ;
Of feathered limb and sturdy frame
Ready to find and spring their game,
Burst forth with glee, and lend their aid
To hunt the woodcock in the glade.
Scattered among the oaks below,
Where hollies and the hazel grow,

The spaniels range with steady care,

And flush the woodcock here and there :

Raised is the tube with fatal aim,

And quick precision wins the game.

But ever and anon 't is found

Tom French has marked a cock to ground ;

And if he point the very spot,

Tom claims a shilling for the shot.

XXXIII

And now to cross the Western Dart

Needs steady eye and practised art ;

Poised on a pinnacle of rock

The hunter springs from block to block ;

And if he hesitates or fears,

Down down he goes o'er head and ears.

From Mousington the vicar came

In search of fish or some such game;

He neared Dart-steps and wished to cross,

But dared not spring on slippery moss;

The parasite had capped the stones

And threatened him with broken bones;

So in he stalked, waist-deep in tide,

And waded to the other side.

For sixty winters, ay and more,

Tom French had crossed from shore to shore;

By night or day, in frost or wet,

His foot had never failed him yet.

As dreary day grows darker still

We cross the stream and breast the hill;

And glowing hearths shine forth again,

A welcome home to dogs and men.

XXXIV

With joy we greet the evening meal,

As hungry men alone can feel;

While other friends have come from far

To join us in the mimic war.

The banquet spread in bounteous ways

Is worthy of Homeric praise;

A loin of beef of knightly size,

A goose that fills the feasting eyes;

A flight of woodcock fresh in store,

And what could hunters wish for more?

But still unsated all would try

The merits of a monster pie:

Six noble cocks had ceased to crow

In Harry's poultry-yard, I know;

Then eggs and ham and all were thrust

Beneath a broad expanse of crust

In platter grand, as Cæsar's dish

Designed for one immortal fish.

Alas! the sumpter 'neath his load

Had stumbled rudely on the road,

And sundry flasks of old Bordeaux

Had burst and soaked the pasty through.

Oh! sad were Harry's feelings moved

To find the compound disapproved;

With double grief his heart was filled,

His wine was lost, his cocks were killed;

The bonnie birds he wished unslain

And crowing in his yard again.

XXXV

In horse-shoe form the party meet

And gather round the glowing peat;

Again, the evening ne'er too long

Is shortened by the tale and song;

And here and there upon the ground

Whimpers a happy dreaming hound:

The pioneers of many a run,

Thus honoured when the chase is done;

While we beguile the night again

With visions of the next campaign.

XXXVI

Exalted to a sylvan throne

' King of the West '* has come from Holne;

* John King, Esq., of Fowelscombe, was long known in the
county of Devon by the title of 'King of the West,' given to

Brimful of heartiness and glee

No pride he knows though King he be :

He tells us tales of many a run,

And decks them with a dash of fun.

Full well the wily fox he knows,

His habits and the point he goes ;

Nor is there on the Western ground

A better judge of horse and hound.

Then out spoke King, on sport intent,

' Trelawny meets at Over-Brent,

' And while I 've life to cross a hack

' I 'll ride to see his brilliant pack.

' Oh for a fox of forest race

' That flies to moor with little grace ;

him in a poem written by his friend Mr. George Templer of
Stover. Mr. King died at the good old age of 73, in his saddle,
on the wild Dartmoor.

E

' That does not dwell until he 's found

' By twang of horn or drawing hound ;

' Like arrow starting from the bow

' With winged flight he seems to go,

' And faith he 'll sorely test the speed

' Of many a noble hound and steed.'

The hope of sport so well expressed

Finds sympathy in every breast ;

And ready is the glad assent

To meet next morn at Over-Brent.

XXXVII

A soft west wind dispels the cloud

That wrapped the moor in dismal shroud ;

And misty curtains melt away

As morning in her mantle grey

Breaks o'er the hills : and clear and high

Fair Ben-shie tor delights the eye:

A wilder scene or lovelier road

Was ne'er by merry hunters trode.

The headlong Dart for ever grand

Encircles it with silver band,

And frets and roars in angry course

Till echoes of the vale are hoarse ;

The granite bars so firm and grey

Are helpless to impede her way:

The torrent now enlarged and bold

The mountain prison fails to hold,

And on she struggles wild to gain

Her freedom in the distant plain.

Gaily across the moorland tracks,

With easy rein and willing hacks,

E 2

We spin along: and soon we find
A broad expanse of moor behind.
Descending now we quickly gain
The limit of the barren plain;
And Over-Brent attracts the eye,
A sidelong cover, high and dry ;
So quiet and so dense, it seems
The very home for Reynard's dreams.

XXXVIII

A bow-shot off or more, I ween,
From cover-side the pack is seen :
As friends from every side appear,
What happy greetings meet the ear.
The Knight of Bradley, ever gay,
Foretells a brilliant scenting day ;

Light-hearted Tom ! whose kindly tongue

With happy joke is ever hung ;

Than he no hunter tops a fence

With stronger nerve, or less pretence ;

And none who join him e'er complain

Of dullness in a Devon *lane.*

Deacon at home on Edgar's back,

With loving eyes surveys the pack ;

' What heads and loins, and limbs below,

' What stamina to stay and go :

' Our Beckford of the West,* I wot,

' Would give this world for such a lot,

' And bribing Charon for his pains

' Would hunt them on Elysian plains.'

* This North-Devon gentleman, perhaps, understands as much, if not more than any man living about

> ' Hounds, and their various breed,
> And no less various use.'—*Somerville.*

Oh ! would that Landseer here had been

To sketch the quiet sylvan scene ;

Or Grant to paint, with finished art,

A *Study* from the banks of Dart.

XXXIX

The bold Carew rejoiced that morn,

To recognise the blood of Quorn ;

For oft he 'd known the desperate pace

Of Green of Rolleston in the chase,

And dreamed that fox of hill or plain

Must yield to hounds of Meynell's strain.

The Beaufort and the Wyndham stud

Had modified the Whimsey blood ;

The Grafton, too, had lent its aid,

In bone and substance well displayed.

With admiration in his eye,

The gallant Radcliffe seemed to sigh,

As though the Warleigh oaks he 'd give

One hour at their sterns to live.

While Limpety* on Jack was proud

To hear 'the beauties' praised aloud.

XL

But now a sound attracts the pack,

The well-known step of some one's hack;

The movements of the stern and ear

Are tokens that a friend is near;

And at the very moment given

Trelawny comes: 'tis just eleven.

* The huntsman Limpety was mounted that day on his
master's celebrated horse Jack Shepherd—than which, over the
moor, a more brilliant hunter was never crossed.

Of manly form and courteous mien,

Scarce fifty summers has he seen ;

And though ' close-buttoned to the chin,'

His heart is warm enough within.

He scans the field with rapid view,

And notes an absent friend or two ;

Though strict to time, he loves to yield

A margin to his tardy field :

' Our distant brothers of the chase

' May claim,' he said, ' a little grace ;

' Where 's Rockingham and brave Bulteel,

' Where Harry Taylor, true as steel ?

' Britons remote, but Britons rare,

' Such men as these we cannot spare.'

XLI

' Ninth Harry ! does he hunt to-day ?'

Said Treby in his hearty way :

' Quite right, Trelawny, give him grace,

' For when he comes he 'll *keep* his place :

' My Eton chum, we held him then

' As Agamemnon, King of Men ;

' And from that sunny day to this

' Taylor has never gone amiss :

' Yes, give him law whose ready hand

' Is always at a friend's command ;

' A kinder heart I never knew,

' So manly, chivalrous, and true.'

Scarce ended were his words, I ween,

Ere Taylor and Bulteel were seen ;

The latter tells what all must know,

That time at Holbeton is slow ;

But Harris thinks the hack is lame,

Though Courtenay's clocks may bear the blame.

XLII

A quiet sign that passes round

Quickens the pulse of every hound;

And scarce they need the mute command

Just given by a wave of hand,

For springing to the cover near

In tangled copse they disappear.

From *Wanderer* one word alone

Announced the fox was up and gone;

A wily beast that held in scorn

The hubbub of the hound and horn,

And ere another tongue had spoke

In stealthy haste away he broke;

A gay Lothario, mad to roam,

Escaping to his distant home.

He flashes from the copse as free

As sunbeam through a waving tree,

An instant, and his golden hue
Is viewed, and then is lost to view.

XLIII

Carew's rich scream, so loud and shrill,
Startles the black-cock on the hill;
It vibrates on the fox's ear,
And every hound has caught the cheer;
It gathers up the scattered pack,
And claps them on his very back;
Then dashing from the cover grey
To moorland hills they bound away.
In piteous tones Trelawny then
Intreats the hard, aspiring men :—
' Pray, gentlemen, restrain your pace,
' Do give my hounds a little space,

' Just room to turn ; pray check your rein,

' Then catch them if you can again.'

Vain is the prayer : 't were easier far

To stem the rolling tide of war :

As soon the winds would stay to hear

Or tarry in their wild career.

But, happily, the pack in speed

At Shipley tor has gained the lead,

And settling to the burning scent

O'er Dock-hill ridge like flames they went.

XLIV

The gallant fox his point to gain

Must fight them on the open plain ;

He never turns a longing look

At Skerraton or Bloody-brook ;

Nor Woolholes does he linger o'er,

The deepest earths in all the moor;

But straight for Holne he flashes by,

A shooting star across the sky;

And if he gain the rocks, I say,

He'll fight those hounds another day!

XLV

Leading the pack and all abreast

At least five couple head the rest;

With killing pace and gallant lead

Dashing and flinging on they speed':

As *Whirligig* is wizzing by,

On very wings he seems to fly;

Now *Nemesis* directs the pack

To vengeance, on the villain's track;

While *Columbine* and *Pantaloon*

Have never tripped to sweeter tune.

XLVI

No fences here ; nor sheep to stain

The pasture of the moorland plain ;

Just now and then a guiding word

From hounds in front is faintly heard ;

A short deep chop is all that 's said

By *Crier*, as he flings ahead ;

Ruby and *Restless*, side by side,

The last on line, the other wide,

With *Beatrice* and *Despot* strain

The laurels of the pack to gain.

Such foxhounds of a noble kind

Would perish ere they lagged behind ;

A glorious feature of the chase,

That struggle for the foremost place.

XLVII

But, gracious Dian, see how far

We 've left the early scene of war ;

There 's Lemson, Skerraton and Skay,

And even Hayford fades away.

Ah ! sore it grieves me to discern

Some noble horsemen far astern ;

Men of undaunted nerve and mind ·

Dotting the moor for miles behind :

Ah ! sadly they bemoan the fate

Of heavy ground and cumbrous weight ;

So good the pace that blood and bone

Are helpless under fifteen stone :

True beasts of burden, faith, are they

Groaning beneath a mass of clay.

XLVIII

A cloud of vapour rolls around
A prostrate form that hugs the ground;
Poole's recent pink that decks his back
Is metamorphosed into black;
His loving wife had died of fright
To see her lord in such a plight.
Sobbing and staggering, here and there,
Are men and beasts in blank despair;
'T was found that horses kept for show
Were horses never meant to go;
Like Pindar's razors made to sell,
They sold, but did not shave so well.

XLIX

But forward still; the straining pack
Are never for an instant slack;

On, like a cataract they pour,

Or hurricane that sweeps the moor;

And now a happy few alone

Are bursting on the wilds of Holne.

But stay; a truce to deadly strife

Just gives the fox a chance of life;

A check ensues; Trelawny then

Implores again the forward men :

' One moment, hold ! yon lad so near

' Has headed back the fox, I fear.'

Then, as a rocket bursts around,

They spread, they fling, they try the ground,

And every horseman holds his breath

At such a point of life or death.

L

But ere the steeds of foremost rank

Had ceased to quiver in the flank :

F

And ere the stooping hounds are led,

In crescent form, to cast ahead,

A hunter views the beaten fox

Stealing away for Whitewood rocks :

' Yonder he goes ; press on the pack ;

' *Ruby* alone is at his back ;

' That jewel, in her brilliant way,

' By forward dash has saved the day.'

And now the hounds, with headlong rush,

Are racing for his very brush ;

And *Destiny* foretells the fate

Impending o'er his sinking state.

No longer like a flash of fire

He shoots o'er mountain, heath, and mire ;

No longer level with his back,

But dark, bedraggled, soiled, and slack,

He bears his brush ; alas ! his bloom

Is quickly changed from light to gloom.

The hounds are on him! aye, 't is o'er,
This wondrous run on old Dartmoor.

LI

No monarch of the world, I trow,
Rejoicing o'er his fallen foe,
Or laden with the battle spoil,
The glory of his blood and toil,
Could estimate Trelawny's bliss
In such a gladsome scene as this.
His panting hounds he stood among,
The centre of a gallant throng;
And as he waved the brush on high,
Contentment beaming from his eye,
He lauds the mettle and the pace
Of every hound that led the chase;
And often from that red-cross day,
In cheery mood he used to say:

F 2

The forward eye and *Ruby's* cast
Had killed the flying fox at last.

LII

Of those in front 't were hard to say
Who led or did not lead the way ;
Suffice it now that, flying o'er,
' The Dactyls' scarcely touched the moor ;
And proud were men in lightning chase
To scan and prove their classic race ;
That Figaro and Cromhall shone
Like glorious stars throughout the run ;
And forward sped the Gainsboro' blood
As freely as a mountain flood.
' Buller of Dean, give me the head ;
· You take the brush,' Trelawny said ;

' Go bear it to your infant boy,

' And deck his cradle with the toy;

' Train him aright, and hope to see

' True scion of your ancient tree;

' Then well I trust he 'll ever court

' The pastime of a manly sport;

' And spite of danger, shoals, and rocks,

' Will steer as straight as this good fox.'

LIII

Not hunters only love to glean

Memorials of a passing scene;

A trifle, as it now appears,

Will touch the heart in after years,

And re-create the scene anew

In colours of a mellow hue.

Slight token, be it leaf or flower,

Will mark for life one blissful hour;

And feelings that were else forgot

Will linger round some cherished spot.

So trophies of the chase recall

The men, the hounds, the steeds and all;

Old friends long gone again appear,

Their welcome voice we seem to hear;

And shadows from the wall depart,

As early sunshine warms the heart.

LIV

Then pleasant thanks the master gains,

A welcome boon for all his pains;

Not smiles and words of doubtful tone,

Meant for the ear and that alone;

Not compliments of guileful art,

Touching the surface, not the heart;

As wintry sun with pallid beam

May gild but cannot warm the stream;

But patent as the light of day

An honest force their words convey.

' Give King his meed,' Trelawny said,

' This noble fox at Holne was bred;

' Sir Walter, too, for covers rare

' Must take of praise the lion's share;

' Buller and him the field will thank

' For covers that are never blank.'

LV

Then Harley spake, a yeoman stout

As ever turned a furrow out:

' Faith, how my wife will carry on

' To hear this fox is dead and gone ;

' Oft has he had,' in spite of guard,

' The pick of all her poultry-yard ;

' Those Dorkings were a heavy blow,

' That won the prize at Totnes show.

' Ah ! long 't will be ere she forgets

' The slaughter of her spangled pets.

' But spite of these nocturnal shocks,

' I grudge the death of such a fox ;

' And hope on future day to find

' The hero's stock is left behind.'

LVI

If Croxton Park can well attest

How Scobell shines in silken vest ;

Well may his practised eye decide
The measure of a horse's stride :
' For six-and-thirty minutes' space
' Methought,' said he, ' I rode a race ;
' I 've known the steeds that could not stay
' At Goodwood, as they 've gone to-day ;
' In truth, the chase was wondrous fast,
' A perfect blaze from first to last.'

LVII

Then slowly o'er the heath and fern
In deep content the hunters turn :
But King, at Holne, would bid them stay
To cheer them on their homeward way.
With eager haste the horses quaffed
The sweet, refreshing, oatmeal draught·

O'er tankards, too, of foaming ale
As rapidly the men prevail;
And many a wreathèd cloud proceeds
In fragrance from Havannah weeds;
The gentle and assuasive leaf
That charms away the stings of grief,
And brings to contemplation's door
A strength she never felt before.

LVIII

O'er moorland path or trackless ways,
Divergent as the solar rays,
In little groups of three or four
The home-bound hunters cross the moor.
The patriot's fire where'er we roam
Burns brightest in an Alpine home;

Stout limbs to do, stout hearts to dare,
Are nurtured by the mountain air.
No marvel 't is that native blood
Is fresh and wild as mountain flood;
No wonder that the mountain race
Have strongest love for native place.
The bleak and barren moor at best
Begets for home a double zest;
The gloom behind, the joy before,
The contrast at the very door;
Its rugged heights but tend to show
The comforts of the vale below;
And all its horrors but endear
The charming homes we find so near.
Bright hearths, and faces brighter far,
Radiant with light as evening star,
Illume and cheer the hunter's breast
With genial warmth and happy zest.

With joys like these so close at hand,

What wonder that he loves the land?

With night so near, and charms in store,   •

No wonder that he leaves the moor.

PART SECOND.

I

WINTER'S away, and long ago
Has laid aside his robe of snow;
And joyous minstrels charm the earth,
At prospect of the Summer's birth.
The sunny copse and Dryad's grove
Are bursting with the songs of love;
On ev'ry side, o'er hill and dale,
The blithe and welcome notes prevail.
The black-cap at the break of day
Trolls sweetly forth his roundelay;
Soft greetings to his native glen
Are pouring from his throat again.
The cuckoo from a distant shore
Returns with joy to old Dartmoor;

And wafted home by gentle winds

A never-failing summer finds.

Like many a worthless spark is he,

Singing his song from tree to tree,

And skimming o'er the flowery meads,

A gay, unsettled life he leads:

Unfettered by domestic care,

He roams for pleasure here and there;

Nor heeds the penalties he 'll pay,

When time has tinged his plumes with grey.

What though no Philomel is near

With plaintive strain to soothe the ear;

The woodlark wild is there to tell

The dulcet tale we love so well;

The passing Zephyr folds his wing

To list the merle and mavis sing;

And Dart, to blend the whole in one,

With gentle murmur ripples on.

II

As echo sleeps, she rolls along,
Mingling her voice with birds of song;
Her margin decked with glorious hue,
A lustre on the waters threw;
And heath, and furze, and yellow broom
Lend to the air a light perfume;
While dew-drops smile on every spray
The jewels of the waking day.
No Eastern monarch ever wore
Such brilliants as her margin bore;
Nor Tempè's vale did e'er unfold
Such beauties to the world of old.
The landscape like a passing dream
Is painted on the fickle stream;
And mirrors in the crystal tide
Reflect again the mountain side.

Not brighter was the silver well,

Where that fond youth Narcissus fell;

Self-love alone was all the sin—

The shadow that enticed him in.

III

With wingèd flight the moments flew,

As Harry and the Celt pursue

Their gentle craft: no time have they

Due homage to the scene to pay.

O'er giant roots and granite blocks,

The refuge of the mountain fox;

They scramble on, absorbed, intent,

Their eyes upon the river bent.

Where'er the gurgling waters tossed,

And ripples curled, but soon were lost;

Or, when Favonius came to aid

And gaily o'er the surface played ;

They wave their pliant rods on high,

And softly cast the painted fly ;

And gently, too, the silk-worm thread

As light as gossamer is spread ;

That scarce the eye can mark withal

Its natural and easy fall.

IV

With eager spring the troutlets rise

To seize the fair delusive prize ;

And quick the little victims pay

The penalty of being gay.

But, now and then, the feathered bait

Attracts a peel of heavy weight,

G

That showing but his dorsal fin
Comes slowly up and gulps it in.
Now good St. Anthony be nigh
And prosper Harry's hand and eye!
See how the line with rapid hiss
Is rushing down a dark abyss:
See how the rod is bent in twain
As Harry turns his fish again.
How wildly now he proves the gear,
Tugging and darting far and near;
And sorely strains the line and rings
As upward in the air he springs:
He strikes for freedom, strong and bold,
But may not, cannot break his hold.

V

Harry at length begins to feel
Less pressure on the creaking reel,

And guides the captive close to land

With steady force and upright hand.

Again he kicks : one struggle more,

And still the fish is not ashore :

With mounted gaff the Celt attends

And o'er the flagging victim bends :

Ah cruel fate ! the pointed steel

Is buried in the dying peel :

Then glittering on the sward he lies,

Quivers awhile—and gasps—and dies.

VI

Oft on the side of that lone stream—

The picture of a poet's dream—

Where fancy in her wildest mood

Might sketch the hill, the moor, the flood :

And varying hues of light and shade

The glories of the vale displayed,

The hunters meet! and oft they stray

Far on its banks the live-long day :

They little heed the prickly gorse

Or granite cleaves that barred their course ;

With all its thorns it seemed to be

A paradise to them and me.

VII

One sunny morn, a peerless day,

When speckled trout refused to play ;

Though Strongshield used his utmost skill

To tempt them up against their will.

He fished the stream so far and fine,

It scarcely felt the falling line ;

And wary troutlets failed to spy

The painted from the real fly ;

For whether red, or blue, or brown,

It dropped as light as thistle-down :

No matter where or what he threw,

In vain was all the art he knew.

At length—for patience has its bound,

And, faith, his stock was not profound—

Strongshield exclaimed : · I 'd like to know

‘ What power holds the fish below :

‘ Either a wind they love the least

‘ Is threatened from the blighting East ;

‘ Or perhaps the scourge of all the race.

‘ The prowling Otter haunts the place ;

‘ I 've tried my luck from either shore

‘ And scarcely ever failed before.’

VIII

The Colt replied : ' Full well I feel

' What joy it is to fill a creel ;

' And well I know if mortal hand

' Success at sport could e'er command,

' That Strongshield's art could never fail

' A bumper in his creel to hail.

' Whate'er the cause, we may not know

' The secrets of the deep below ;

' With wind at East and sun so bright

' The fishing day is never right :

' So yield to fate ; nor risk your fame

' In playing at a losing game.

' To-morrow at the dawn of day

' " *Midnight*" and " *Prince*" shall guide the way

· And if an Otter scourge the stream

' They 'll rouse him from his soundest dream ;

' And sore he 'll pay the felon's smart

' For ravaging the banks of Dart.'

IX

' Bravo !' cried Fitz, whose Devon race

Were famous for the love of chace,

' To-morrow from his rocky lair

' We 'll bolt the beast in wild despair;

' And when he seeks the tide in vain

' We 'll drive him to his holt again.

' But come ; the shaggy, distant moor

· Has many marvels still in store ;

' Let 's stride away a southern course,

' Where Yealm and Erme have kindred source ;

' Where welling from the womb of earth

' The new-born waters struggle forth :

' Or compass-led we 'll seek alone

' The Abbott's way and Peter's stone.'

X

Then governed as by one consent

O'er many a brook and moss they went ;

Now scouring o'er the flowery ling,

The blackcock shows his mottled wing :

And as they cross the peaty waste,

The curlew quits the scene in haste ;

The peewit flaps along the ground,

Or wheels in endless circles round ;

The breeding snipe is soaring high,

Drumming his grief beneath the sky.

And harpy-like, not far away,

The buzzard watches o'er his prey ;

With piercing eye and rapid flight
He skims the moor from morn till night;
The feathered tribe are mute with dread
At visage of his hoary head ;
And fiercely here he seems to reign
The pirate of the marshy plain.

XI

Then, as they watch the wild birds' ways,
A distant form attracts their gaze ;
They pause awhile, and faintly scan
The outline of a horse and man,
As looming 'twixt the earth and sky
He picked his way with wary eye ;
Fool-hardy to the last degree,
Or mazed at least the man must be.

Here, where the demon lights his fire,
And flickers wildly o'er the mire,
Leading the stranger, lost and late,
Bewildered to his lonesome fate;
The man, confiding in his horse,
With safety keeps a forward course,
And guides him with a gentle hand
Where instinct points the firmest land.
In sight the Pits of Erme appear,
For which the horseman seems to steer;
And thither, as by happy chance,
The hunters one and all advance.

XII

Emerging from the miry ground,
With step elastic on they bound,

As though their limbs were glad to gain
The freedom of the heather plain.
Soon they approach the broken soil,
The work of many a year of toil;
Where, ages back, the miner's hand
With hollow grips had scored the land :
Sheltered and sunk below the moor,
What cover here for rifle-corps !
A whole brigade might safely lie
Secluded from the keenest eye.
Though still afar, the friends survey
A long and low flea-bitten grey;
Bearing a man of twelve-stone weight
With easy step and steady gait;
The clean-cut head and swelling vein
Imply a dash of Arab strain :
Tough and enduring seemed the steed
For longest run or utmost need.

XIII

The rider as he nears the scene

Appears of rough and ready mien ;

As though he did not care a groat

What people said or people thought.

His flowing locks might just betray

Faint touches of incipient grey,

While freely in the summer wind

They float in tresses far behind—

In homely, unadorned attire,

Befitting well the bog or brier,

Those careless robes at least confess

A pure contempt for modern dress.

In outward form he might have been

The Mohican of that wild scene ;

Rough-hewn he seemed, and free to roam

The guardian of his forest home.

XIV

At first the puzzled hunters scan

The rude exterior of the man ;

But, as the bark may never be

The proof of worth within the tree ;

Nor may the rugged surface show

The treasures of the mine below ;

Instead of some Bœotian boor,

A son of earth, and nothing more ;

How great their joy, as nigh he drew,

To grasp the hand of one they knew—

A hand that in the sight of heaven

Without his heart was never given.

XV

' Though oft,' he said, 'I 've wandered o'er

' This wild and unfrequented moor,

‘ I 've rarely seen a native cross

‘ Yon hollow, dark, and faithless moss ;

‘ But, fleetly o'er the mire you came,

‘ As light as Jack-o'-lantern's flame ;

‘ For pace and dash, in very sooth,

‘ Give me again the blood of youth.'

XVI

‘ We hoped,' said Vesey, ‘ here to trace

‘ Some relics of that Celtic race,

‘ Which, delving for a precious ore,

‘ With rugged marks has scarred the moor.

‘ So, glancing from the western Dart,

‘ The sky above our only chart,

‘ O'er heath and sedge, and brooklets gay,

‘ Just as a heron wings his way,

' We steered a random course, 't is true,

' And happily have met with you.'

XVII

' I doubt, indeed, if here you find

' The footsteps of the British kind;

' For miners shrewd of later day

' Have delved and borne the wealth away;

' And left these barren pits to form

' A covert from the pelting storm.

' Besides,' said he, with meaning eye,

' Some living treasures here may lie;

' O'er which in spite of desert plain,

' The fair Lucina loves to reign.'

XVIII

' Beyond the haunts of busy men,

' Beyond the keeper's deadly ken,

' A little vixen near this ground

' A happy quiet home has found ;

' And ne'er has failed for many a year

' Some stout and healthy cubs to rear :—

' But nightly still she need to stray

' Long weary miles to seek her prey ;

' And oft, methinks, the raid is scant

' And ill supplies the litter's want.

' So, to the hen-wife's serious grief,

' Our poultry-yard affords relief ;

' For many a crested cock will droop

' A sacrifice to fatal croup ;

' Or barren hens the cause befriend

· By coming to untimely end.

' My saddle-bag e'en now contains

' A very ancient cock's remains ;

' And faith, I do not care to know

' Whether he fell by pest or blow ;

'Enough for me : 't will serve to brace

'The litter for the future chase.'

XIX

The hunters then confess to feel

True horror of the Dorset steel ; *

And fervently their views impart

Anent the Vulpecidal art :

Sweet words are they, that seem to rest

Like balm upon the rider's breast—

But when the hunters sought to know

If foxes were the shepherd's foe,

And if, like wolves, they snatch away

The lambkins as they skip and play,

They touched upon a tender string

That seemed his very soul to wring.

* A destructive gin, said to be invented by a Dorsetshire keeper.

II

XX

'Foul slander that, as ever came

'In malice from the throat of Fame;

''Think you,' said he, 'in this wild spot,

'Where human aid avails them not;

'Where, heather-born, no ear is nigh

'To note their feeble infant cry:

'Where shelter in the fern and rocks

'Is shared alike by lambs and fox;

'If once a fox by hunger led,

'The blood of lambs had fiercely shed,

'That e'er again that fox would stay

'His havoc on the helpless prey?

'Ah no! the beast would soon be found

'The terror of the country round;

'The slayer would destroy by scores

'His victims on the lonely moors;

' And every farmer then might fear

' The devastation far and near.'

XXI

The subject, as he ceased to speak,

With sparks of fire dashed his cheek,

And showed by that expressive touch

He 'd fight for those he loved so much.

Then pointing to a distant mound

That seemed to crown the desert round :

' Thither I go,' he said, ' to share

' A portion of my baggage fare ;

' Another litter yonder lies

' That sorely needs these scant supplies :

' This rook that robbed our early wheat

' Will serve them for a glorious treat ;

H 2

' They 'll pluck his wings, and pick his bones,

' And romp, like kittens, round the stones ;

' As fair a sight as e'er was seen

' That pastime on their native green.'

XXII

   Then from his lips there briefly fell

For each and all a kind farewell ;

He and the long flea-bitten grey

With gentle motion glide away,

And soon again are dimly traced,

Strange features in that forest waste.

Alas ! since then long years have passed,

Checking the hunters' pace at last,

And leaving tracks upon their brow

Of thought and care, and locks of snow,

That o'er their temples thinly wave
As blossoms of a future grave.

XXIII

The hunters oft recall with pain
The form they ne'er may see again;
They miss the fine patrician face
That charmed the board, or cheered the chase;
They miss the hearty words he flung
With vigour from his classic tongue;
And old Dartmoor, in accents wild,
Will long lament her much-lovèd child.
Braced by a pure and mountain air,
She reared him with a mother's care;
And gently, on her rugged breast,
She soothed him when he sank to rest.

For ever widowed and bereft

Her lonely side the man has left;

And now the dark and pensive moor

Is darker than it was before;

While he, on soaring wings of flight,

Has changed it for a land of light.

XXIV

Once more at Brimpts; in happy strain

The hunters tell their tales again;

In swifter current flows the blood,

At incidents of field and flood.

The rider and his speckled grey

Are social food for many a day;

The vision of the lonely plain

In fancy floats across the brain;

Though lost to sight, it still is nigh,

Like sculpture that has charmed the eye.

Perversely some affect to doubt

The distance of the morning route,

And earnestly assure the rest

That Yealm's true head was farther west;

That scatheless none might dare to cross

The precincts of that spongy moss,

Whence Yealm, escaping, wins its way

From darkness to the light of day;

Uncertain still, they doubt and smile,

Like sceptics at the source of Nile.*

XXV

The granite pile of Crockern tor,

The council hall of peace or war,

* Captains Speke and Grant have at length solved this problem.

Attracts the few, who love to pore

On records of the ancient moor;

And fancy now delights to stray

O'er legends of an early day;

When British chiefs, in painted guise,

Dispensed the law beneath the skies;

And wild, unlettered natives got

Rude justice from the hallowed spot.

Or, haply, when at later date

The courtly Rawleigh sat in state;

And held the balance, firm and fair,

Enthroned upon that granite chair;

Lord-Warden here; on metal bright

He judged the royal maiden's right;

And Stannators a hundred strong

Proclaimed the cause of right or wrong.

But now, of all that busy train,

The silent rocks alone remain;

And Crockern tor now seems to stand
The Sinai of that desert land.

XXVI

Another guest had gleaned a store
Of lichens on the rocky moor;
Strange parasites that well supply
The colours of the Tyrian dye.
Like Israel's king he seemed to be
Curious in every plant and tree,
And told us, in inviting mood,
Of wonders seen at Wistman's wood;
Where stunted oaks of hideous form
Lie shrinking from the western storm;
The gaunt and shrivelled limbs are spread
Like spectres' arms above the dead;

As if with blighted hope they prayed
Removal from that sterile glade.

XXVII

Scarce six feet high, for ages past
Their heads have borne the wintry blast;
But dominant o'er stem and bole
The pendant moss usurps the whole;
And haply thus the pigmy race
Has dwindled 'neath its close embrace:
The long funereal tresses wave
Like willows o'er a parent's grave;
Such dismal, hoary beards have they,
Those patriarchs of the forest grey—
And when, with sad and fitful sigh,
The misty wind is coursing by,

LIVE DRUIDS.

In tattered robes and dismal guise
Strange goblin figures seem to rise.
Here stands a chief with nodding plume,
Desponding o'er his silent doom ;
And there, at eve, to fancy's ken,
The Druid's form is seen again.

XXVIII

Freely the speaker loved to pore
On superstition's darkest lore ;
But freer far his thoughts pursue
Old Nature in her wildest hue ;
Seeking a fern he 'd wander round
From Dunnabridge to old Grimspound ;
Or stride away o'er bog and fell
To sound the depths of Clacey-well.

His fairest bouquet, culled in spring,
Was cotton-grass and purple ling;
And oft the honey-bee would note
The sweets that decked his morning coat;
And blithely humming, seek to share
A portion of its stolen fare.
But hark! in deep and mellow strain
The tuneful chord is touched again;
And Harry's thrilling notes relate
The tale of faithful Gelert's fate;
How Prince Llewellyn rued the blow
That laid the noble creature low;
And wakeful echoes sadly tell
How Snowdon wept when Gelert fell.
Then scarcely dies the loud applause
That Harry's touching ballad draws,
When, in his turn, the Celt sustains
The spirit of the vocal strains.

SONG.

THE RUGGED DARTMOOR.

Let Fashion exult in her giddy career,

And headlong her course through the universe steer;

There 's a land in the West never bowed to her throne,

Where Nature for ages has triumphed alone,

And Dian oft revels in wild extacy

O'er gray granite tors or soft mossy lea,

Where the fox loves to kennel, the buzzard to soar,

All boundless and free o'er the rugged Dartmoor.

Tradition still lingers her legend to tell

Of Hunter benighted by Pixie and spell,

When, an-hunger'd and cold, in his uttermost need,

His hand was imbrued in the blood of his steed,

And the hollow recess, for shelter and heat,

Disembowell'd presents a welcome retreat ;

But, alas ! on the morrow, encrusted in gore,

He was found a stiff corse on the rugged Dartmoor.*

Of ages long past here are relics, I ween,

Where Cursus and Cromlech † preside o'er the scene ;

Humanity shudders the altars to trace,

Where rites of the Druid a fiend would disgrace :

E'en History blushes their deeds to unfold,

And Fancy has furnished the sequel untold,

For the genius of Bray and Carrington's lore

Have gilded thy stories, thou rugged Dartmoor.

---

* The well-known story of Childe, the Plymstock hunter, who was found frozen to death inside his steed.

† Cursus, the Via Sacra of the Druids. — Cromlech, their Altar, on which they immolated human victims.

But farther to search in Antiquity's page

I leave to the worm-eaten brains of the Sage.

Enamour'd of Nature, her charms I revere

In creatures of life on the mountain and mere;

The jetty blackcock and the watchful curlew,

The loud booming bittern and harrier so blue.

Oh! the plover's wild scream and the cataract's roar

Are the sounds that I love on the rugged Dartmoor.

Unrivall'd in beauty and kennell'd in rocks,

As King of the Forest I honour the fox;

He recks not of law, and he plunders amain

Whatever is dainty on hill-side or plain :

As wild as the winds and as swift his career,

'T is a sharp pack will carry this bold buccaneer;

But vengeance, though tardy, will come to his door,

And his doom be denounced on the rugged Dartmoor.

Near Hen-tor's gray covert a crash might be heard,

(But, mark you, those horsemen say never a word,)

Yet it thrills through the heart and it fires the eye

Both of rider and horse as the sound hurries by :

That crash tells 'the Find,' and they view with delight

The fox flashing by like a meteor at night ;

With blood, bone, and mettle, they 'll prove him full sore

Ere he gain Ben-shie tor * on the rugged Dartmoor.

As a pilot o'ertaken by storms on the sea

Now scuds with the gale for a port on his lee ;

So the bold buccaneer with a pack at his stern

Steals on for his point through heather and fern :

He passes the mires of Fox-tor and Plym,

Where the steeds struggle through, and all sob but him :

* The fatal Ben-shie's boding scream.
Lady of the Lake, 3 Canto Stan. 7.

Ten couple of hounds view him home to his door,

As he GAINS Ben-shie tor on the rugged Dartmoor.

The homeward-bound hunter, with stars for his guide,

Now beams at the thoughts of his own fireside,

And socially presses the stranger to share

With hearty kind welcome the best of his fare;

And if hospitality ever can cheer,

The gloom of the forest enhances it here :

Though bleak be the wind there are comforts in store,

For warm are the hearths near the rugged Dartmoor.

Far removed be the day ere Fashion deface

The features and charms of this primitive place !

May her schemes prove abortive, by ruin dispersed,

And force the pet-bubble of Science* to burst !

* Pet-bubble—*quasi*, the boiler of the steam engine.

I

The Freehold of Nature, though rugged it be,

Long, long may it flourish unsullied and free !

May the fox love to kennel, the buzzard to soar,

As tenants of Nature on rugged Dartmoor.

XXIX

The God of light, in silver car,

Has climbed the hills of distant Yar;

And on the mountain-top is born

The fragrant, dewy, smiling morn :

A few soft clouds above her play

As sponsors for the future day ;

And underneath are freshly spread

The dew-drops that bedeck her bed.

The ruddy cock has clapped his wings,

And loud his grateful matin rings ;

While deep-mouthed hounds rejoice to pay

Their welcome to the God of day.

That country-sound, so sweet and clear,

With magic touch salutes the ear,

Uplifts the heart, unlocks the eyes,

And bids the waking hunters rise ;

Inviting sounds that seem to say

Come to the woodlands, come away.

XXX

Uproused the hunters, one and all,

Responsive to the gladsome call

Their couches quit ; and then, I ween,

A lively skirmish marks the scene ;

Loud shouts arise ! the rafters ring

For water from the bubbling spring :

In feeling notes the men bewail
The scant supply of tub and pail;
And now a missing tub is made
The object of a morning raid;
And fortunate is he who gains
His early plunge at any pains.
Forthwith enveloped for the chase
Soft, fleecy hose their limbs encase,
Such garments from the banks of Tweed
As forest hunters well may need.

XXXI

Then on the sparkling river-side
The mottled hounds are spreading wide;
With curious sense, above, below,
They stem the torrent to and fro.

ON THE DART.

Now by the rapids wildly tossed,
And now in gurgling eddies lost,
They wind alike with steady care
The running stream and tainted air.
Each dark recess and caverned hole,
Each hanging bank and willow bole,
In every nook they seek to trace
The tyrant of the finny race.

XXXII

Then from the rugged granite shore
The very welkin seems to roar;
They hit a trail; and every hound
Is welcomed by the rocks around;
As echo from her wild retreat
The joyous challenge seems to greet,

A thousand tongues at once agree

To swell the sylvan harmony;

While old impending cliffs maintain

The honours of the chase again.

Like music on a marriage morn

Is that sweet note of hound and horn;

With it the blending waters roll

To charm the sense and cheer the soul.

Oh ! had the Syrens ever sung

With half so sweet and fair a tongue,

Penelope had sighed in vain

To see her hero home again.

XXXIII

The swelling music now appears

To fall upon enchanted ears :

But, hunters, hold ! a moment, hark !

Yon hounds proclaim a solid mark.

The terriers too are close before

Hard knocking at the felon's door ;

Hot quarters for the knave, I trow,

But give him room, and ' look below ! '

See there he bolts ! a loud ' heugh-gaze '

His quick and stealthy course betrays !

Then to the surface rise amain

The bubbles in a silver chain ;

The hounds in chase, without delay,

In wild excitement plunge away ;

Catching the scent that seems to glide

In floating fragrance down the tide.

XXXIV

But stay ! the current bears the pack

Headlong beyond the otter's track ;

Now sound the horn and gently guide

The steady hounds on either side;

And casting upward here and there,

With patient toil the fault repair.

Now list! the wild ecstatic strain

Is bursting from the hounds again;

Unerring notes that clearly show

Fresh tidings of the lurking foe.

Again he bolts; again he flies;

And vainly every hover tries.

As pirates of the Eastern main

A peaceful harbour seldom gain,

While British cruisers swift pursue

The dark, relentless, bloody crew.

'T is thus with him; where'er he steer,

No peace he finds, no refuge near.

XXXV

The frequent bubbles now ascend,

Prophetic of his coming end ;

See ! there he lands ; and now the pack

Are crashing on his very track ;

Vain is the tangled copse to hide

The tyrant of the glassy tide ;

And vain the old frequented haunt

To save him in his utmost want.

The dark avengers close astern

Are pressing on at every turn ;

When suddenly the joyous cry

In muffled music seems to die.—

And now the wild and sylvan roar

Is hushed upon the silent shore ;

And frantic echoes now are still

That waked the peaceful, slumbering hill ;

They have him fast! good hounds, well done;

The gallant prize is fairly won.

Then loud resounding, far and free,

Beneath a trembling aspen tree ;

Men, hounds and terriers, one and all,

With joy proclaim the felon's fall.

XXXVI

If ever mortals could pursue

A pastime of a venial hue,

Or earthly charms could e'er bestow

A pure enjoyment here below,

The chase alone may fairly claim

Precedence in the stirring game.

The fairest rose, the honey bee,

Are not from thorns and venom free ;

And bright-eyed faces often dart

An arrow that enslaves the heart.

But, where's the man can ever say,

That, looking back, he rued the day,

When pastime of a guiltless kind

Engaged his thought and cheered his mind ?

No thorns Diana's roses bring,

The honey comes without the sting ;

And many a faithless fair will yield

Her triumphs on this battle-field.

XXXVII

Beyond the roar of busy life,

Beyond the crowded city's strife :

Far from the gilded salons gay,

Where vices thrive, and men decay,

The happy hunter seeks to earn

His pastime on the lonely burn;

Or in some deep sequestered dell

Pursues the chase he loves so well;

Where Nature's bounteous loving-cup

With grateful joy is brimming up.

No venom in that flowing bowl

Is lurking there to kill the soul;

But fountains ever fresh and clear

Supply the hunter round the year.

And when the chase is fairly o'er,

How joyously he quits the moor:

Aye! home to him may well bestow

Its gleam of sunshine here below;

And give him, with its rest and love,

An earnest of the home above.

NOTES.

NOTES.

' Far in Devonia's favoured land
Extends a forest wild and grand.'

We learn from Mr. Rowe that, according to a report laid on the table of the House of Commons, Dartmoor contains 130,000 acres; but this calculation must include adjoining wastes and certain manors which do not properly belong to the Forest of Dartmoor. Its average level rises from 1,400 to 2,000 feet above the sea; its length is estimated at twenty, and its breadth at from twelve to fourteen miles. Mr. R. J. King, in his interesting work on Dartmoor, says:—'From the very earliest period, the tract of wild land which forms the actual forest appears to have been in the power of the Crown. It is the opinion of Mr. Kemble, the learned editor of the *Anglo-Saxon Charters*, that the King succeeded the heathen priests as the rightful possessor of all the waste lands in the kingdom. During the struggles of the Saxon Kings with the retreating Britons, Dartmoor seems to have been but little regarded, except as far as its rocks and glens might have afforded shelter to the enemy, and, possibly, as a district from which tin might be obtained; but after the

Conquest, it became an important hunting ground; and when, in 1203, King John disafforested all the rest of Devon and Cornwall, his right to retain the royal "forests" of Dartmoor and Exmoor was unquestioned and undisputed. Ever since the Conquest, Dartmoor appears to have formed a portion of the grants from the Crown to the Earldom of Cornwall; in which the City and Castle of Exeter are also included. There was, according to Manwood, an ancient belief, not, however, he tells us "of any good ground or authoritie," that the King alone could rightfully possess, as he alone could create, a forest. For this reason, perhaps, it is occasionally referred to as the Chase of Dartmoor, and more than once as Lydford Chase, from the Castle of Lydford, at which the forest courts were held. But at such times as the Earldom of Cornwall has been in abeyance, its revenues, including those derivable from the stannaries and fines of Dartmoor, have reverted to the Crown; and this has been the case sufficiently often for it to retain, for the most part, its royal title of "forest." It must be remembered, also, that the Norman and Anglo-Saxon Earls of Cornwall succeeded to the rights of the old British Princes — a fact which will account for some of their most important privileges.'

Note 2.   Page 3.

' And bear upon their bosom-tide
A world of commerce far and wide.'

The five principal rivers which rise on Dartmoor are the Plym, the Dart, the Tavy, the Teign, and the Taw: all of which are

fine salmon streams, and expand into safe and capacious harbours. In addition to these, there are at 'least twenty-four
secondary rivers, fifteen brooks, besides many without names,
two lakes, and seven heads; or altogether fifty-three streams.'
Thus Devon, from Dartmoor alone, would be eminently entitled
to her old Celtic name of Deuff-neynt, or the land of deep
brooks.

Note 3. Page 3.

'*The giant tors approach the skies.*'

Col. Mudge, in his *Trigonometrical Survey of Devon*, enume-
rates above one hundred tors, all of which still bear their
ancient and distinctive names.

Note 4. Page 7

'*Druids and Celts have passed away,
The Priests and Pagans of the day.*'

Mr. Godfrey Higgins, in his work on *The Celtic Druids*, says,
'By a comparison of the alphabets of different nations, I have
succeeded in showing that the Celtæ and Druids must have come
to this country more than 1,500 years before Christ.'—Ch. v.
sect. 1.

Note 5. Page 9.

'*Old Nature's impress marks the moor
From Heytor to the Western shore.*'

The following graphic sketch of its scenery is thus given by

K

Mr. King:—'It is the wide extent of these solitary wastes which makes them so impressive, and gives them their influence over the imagination. Whether seen at mid-day, when the gleams of sunlight are chasing one another along the hill-side ; or at sunset, when the long line of dusky moorland lifts itself against the fading light of the western sky, the same character of extent and freedom is impressed on the landscape, which carries the fancy from hill to hill, and from valley to valley, and leads it to imagine other scenes of equal wildness, which the distant hills conceal

"Beyond their utmost purple rim."

Perhaps the scenery of Dartmoor is never more impressive than under those evening effects which have last been suggested. The singular shapes, assumed by the granite cappings of the tors, are strongly projected against the red light of the sunset, which gleams between the many openings in the huge pile of rock, making them look like passages into some unknown country beyond them, and suggesting that idea of infinity, which "is afforded by no other object in an equal degree." Meanwhile the heather of the foreground is growing darker and darker ; and the only sound which falls upon the ear is that of the river far below, or, perhaps, the flapping of some heron's wings, as he rises from his rock in the stream, and disappears westward ;

" Where darkly painted on the blood-red sky,
His figure floats along ——"'

Note 6.   Page 10.

' Than fair Dart-meet full well I ween,
A sweeter spot was never seen.'

' A tribe of gipsies has for a long period established itself during the summer on Dartmoor, passing the winter months in the villages on its borders. Their favourite resting place is at Dart-meet, on the immediate boundary of the forest ; and whether the " tribes of the wandering foot " be or be not alive to the wild beauties of the country over which they roam, whoever may look down on Dart-meet of a clear autumn evening, when twilight is slowly closing, will readily admit that a more picturesque spot for their encampment could hardly have been selected.'—KING's *Dartmoor.*

Note 7.   Page 15.

' Ah ! well I mind the gladsome morn,
When Strongshield with his hounds and horn.'

' Forte scutum salus Ducum,' the well-known motto of the Fortescue family, is traceable to the battle of Hastings. On that glorious occasion, which gave to England the most enlightened and the most chivalrous race in Europe to be her kings and rulers, ' Sir Richard de Forte, a man of extraordinary strength and courage, and an eminent soldier, bore a strong shield before William Duke of Normandy, at the great battle of Hastings, against King Harold, where the Duke had three horses killed under him. In which great danger and conflict Sir

Richard de Forte was of great safety to the Norman Duke; from whence the motto "Forte scutum salus Ducum," the scutum, or seu, being added to the name of Forte composeth the name Fortescue. In this fight was also Sir Adam Fortescue, his son, who was a great commander, and behaved himself so well that, for the good services which he and his father Sir Richard had done, the Conqueror gave him Wimstone, in the parish of Modbury, in the county of Devon, and with it many other lands in Devon and other counties. After this kingdom was settled, Sir Richard returned to Normandy. Sir Adam was the first of Wimstone House.' The present Mr. W. B. Fortescue, of Fallapit, the lineal descendant of the shield-bearing hero, still holds property conferred upon his ancestor by the great Conqueror himself.

Note 8.   Page 16.

' *The sport ambitious riders spoil*
  Would cause his Norman blood to boil.'

It is a very common practice among jealous riders, to over-ride the scent, and so to spoil their own sport as well as that of others. Strongshield as a master of hounds was by no means singular in his objections to such a proceeding.

Note 9.   Page 29.

' *Fixed and intent, with heron eye,*
  A fish at work he seems to spy.'

' It has been generally supposed that the male salmon, during the spawning season, assists the female in forming the spawning-bed. This idea is, I think, founded in error, as, during the whole course of my experience, I have never been able to detect the male taking any share whatever in the more laborious portion of these parental duties. The female, regardless of the occasional absence of the males, proceeds with her operations by throwing herself, at intervals of a few minutes, upon her side, and while in that position, by the rapid action of her *tail*, she digs a receptacle in the gravel for her ova, a portion of which she deposits, and, again turning upon her side, she covers it up by a renewed action of the tail — thus, alternately digging, depositing, and covering ova, until the process is completed by the laying of the whole mass, an operation which generally occupies three or four days.'—From Mr. Shaw's Paper, as quoted by Mr. Yarrell in his able work on *British Fishes*.

Note 10. Page 33.

'The swift prolific stream should yield
Its treasures like a fertile field.'

Mr. Frank Buckland, in a very interesting lecture on Pisciculture, which he lately delivered at the Royal Institution, says: 'The French consider that water may be so cultivated as to be more valuable than land, but we have greatly neglected it. Ladies and gentlemen, when we consider the wonderful fecundity of fish, it is perfectly astonishing that our waters are not filled with them. Now, a bird makes a nest, and she lays her eggs in it.

I am told that it is a good fowl that will lay 120 eggs in a year, but fishes lay eggs by the thousand. The eggs of fish are contained in what is called the roe, and all of us who indulge in the matutinal herring know what a *hard* roe is: it is neither more nor less than a dense mass of thousands of eggs. Now when the fish lays its eggs it scoops a long trough out in the gravel, deposits its eggs in the gravel and covers them over with the gravel; and here I present you with specimens of the roes of various fish, each roe contained in a separate bottle, and the number of eggs in each. These results have all been weighed, and a proportion counted out by a young lady, and afterwards calculated out by a young gentleman, Mr. Heap, who I need not say is very clever at figures. As I never trust books when I can get specimens, they were kindly, at my request, supplied me by Mr. Grove, of Charing-cross, and by Mr. Townsend of King William Street. I prepared them myself, and this is the result:

	Weight.	Eggs.
Salmon	1lb	1,000*
Trout	1lb	1,008
Perch	$\frac{1}{2}$lb	20,592
Roach	$\frac{3}{4}$lb	480,480
Smelt	2oz	36,652
Lump fish	2lb	116,640
Brill	4lb	239,775
Herring	$\frac{1}{2}$lb	19,840

* Tables shown as ascertained by Mr. Buist, at Stormontfield, showing 1,000 eggs to the pound.

	Weight.		Eggs.
Jack	. . . . . 4½lb	. . . . . .	42,840
Mackarel	. . . . 1lb	. . . . . .	2,670
Turbot	. . . . 8lb	. . . . . .	385,200
Cod	. . . . . . 20lb	. . . . . .	4,872,000

Now with all this immense number of eggs, how is it that the rivers and seas are not swarmed with fish? I will tell you. It is because of the immense number of enemies the ova has, and which prey upon them, so that I am informed on the best authority, that but one single salmon ovum in every thousand ever produces a fish fit for human food.'

Note 11.   Page 38.

' And if to Foxtor mires he roam
He 'll bid a long adieu to home.'

During the winter months the moor is very frequently enveloped by a dark wet fog; then woe be to the most experienced hunter if he wander from the beaten path. There is a remarkable line of single stones which stretches for a considerable distance across the moor, and passes the very brink of some of the most dangerous mires: it is called the Abbott's way, and is supposed to have been marked out by the monks in their perilous passages across the moor from Buckfast Abbey to that of Tavistock.

Note 12. Page 41.

' Tom's glint of eye was such, I ween,
As in a fox alone is seen.'

The following notice of the death of poor Tom French, of Dartmoor, was communicated by the author of *Dartmoor Days* to the *Exeter Gazette* of January 1858 :—

' To many of our readers, not only in this and the adjoining counties, but even to sojourners in the far-distant towns of Cirencester, York, and Waterford, the termination of Tom French's earthly career will be a subject of considerable interest and much regret. At length the mighty hunter has himself gone to ground, and paid the last debt of nature at the toll-bar of eternity — the grave — to him, of whom he loved to tell :

My name is Death, oh do n't you see
Lords, dukes, and ladies bow down to me.

To him, who bestrides the pale charger and who cuts down all who breathe the breath of life, the veteran has at last succumbed. The sickle has been put in, and the sheaf has been gathered, hoary and ripe for harvest.

' Let us hope that the eighty-four winters which he passed among the wilds of the rugged Dartmoor will be followed by summers of eternal rest and sunshine.

' Born and bred on Dartmoor, and devoted to the charms of the chase, he knew every bog and tor from Bellivor to Durestone ; nay, it is scarcely too much to say that he knew every holt and hover which could harbour a fox or an otter between Heytor Rock and Tolchmoor Gate.

'After being for some years in domestic service, he settled in Widdecombe, and here it was that his remarkable capabilities for the chase were first actively displayed. A popular 'squire of the county,* who, like Cæsar, could do three things at once, paint two distinct subjects with his right and left hands and dictate a business letter all at the same time, is said to have driven his carriage in hot haste to a convenient spot, thrown open its doors and emancipated a host of French and English foxes on the wilds of Dartmoor. As caged animals are always the most mischievous when they regain their liberty, so these were not improved by their temporary captivity. The poor man's goose on the common was no longer safe, and even the farmers' hen-roosts in Widdecombe were assailed with no ordinary daring and ferocity. A council was soon called; and the hero of this memorial, poor Tom French, was the Sir Colin Campbell fixed upon in the country's emergency. Accordingly, a war of retaliation commenced, and Tom with a handful of hounds and a few irregular terriers pursued the villains with remorseless rigour; his motto being to "spare neither sex nor age," for, said he, "'t is a nasty varmint, and aufght to be killed on the Sabbath as well as on the week-day."

'But when, after a long and successful campaign, the ranks of the enemy had been thoroughly thinned and subdued, Tom's occupation became a precarious one; and the farmers, no longer

---

* Mr. John C. Bulteel.

fearing an invasion, ungratefully withdrew the supplies upon which Tom's very existence depended. A few well-timed presents now dropped in from the members of a neighbouring hunt; Tom, ill used by his quondam friends, renounced the destructive system, and was ever after, as he professed to be, a follower of the gen'lemen's sport by inclination as well as practice. Notwithstanding the loss of his right thumb, occasioned by the bursting of a gun, in "shooting to a horny-wink," Tom threw a fly with a fine and delicate hand; a dish of fresh trout for breakfast was always procurable when he was at hand; when the water was too clear and the fish would not come to him, Tom sharpened his cutlass, or rather shouldered his spurt-net, and went in at them.

'The glint of Tom's eye was that of the fox itself, nevertheless, with the expression of cunning on the surface, still there was a clear and strong current of candour beneath. No man was ever better company; he told a story with a ready wit and marvellous humour: "Tom, you've told us what you can do, now just tell us what you can't do," said a gentleman one day, bantering him. "That's easily done, sir," said he, "I can *spend* a five-pound note as well as any man, but I can't *make* one, which, I believe, your honour can." The gentleman was a well-known banker, and the counter-hit provoked a thunder of applause. It need scarcely be added that the glint of Tom's eye was more than usually significant on that occasion.

'The tops of the granite rocks which lie imbedded in the angry Dart bore the impress of Tom's foot for many a year;

for he, and the otter, and the water-ouzel, were the only animals which displaced the mossy-cap with which they were
covered. At the age of seventy-two his activity in crossing the
Dart, by bounding from stone to stone, and pitching exactly on
the summit of each, was quite wonderful, and puzzled and
soused many an athletic follower. On one occasion, in particular, Tom and a fishing-party had crossed the steps of the
swollen-river, below Dart-meet, but the Rector of Mousington,
a young and agile man, fearing a back-fall, walked deliberately
into the water, and waded waist-deep through the angry flood.

'About the period of Christmas, for the last few years, Tom
was in the habit of descending from his native hills, and spend-
ing a week or two with the gen'lemen at their own homes, and
he never came empty-handed. Two or three fat geese, slung
over his back *à la reynard*, were the usual acceptable presents
by which he was accompanied. During his stay at 'Squire
Strongshield's, of Valley-pool, or at his still no less hospitable
brother's, the rector of the parish, Tom found a warm and hearty
welcome from all; "the room" rung with merriment, and the
children and servants were always charmed with his company.
He used to say that somehow or other his waistcoat seemed
to fit him much better after than before these visits. But he
never tarried long away from his native tors; like the carrier-
pigeon, his thoughts were always turned towards home. "I
would rather live," said he, "in the hollow rocks of Blacky-
tor, than in the finest house in Plymouth."

'Every member of "the happy Brimpts' meetings" is in-
debted to poor Tom for many a good day's sport, and for the

enjoyment of many a cheerful evening. The remembrance of
him will long be cherished by his many friends, not one of
whom will ever look upon those piles of primæval rocks without
thinking, "What an appropriate and glorious monument would
a tor be, dedicated to the memory of poor Tom French," a
monument,

Quod non imber edax, non Aquilo impotens
Possit diruere ——

'DIRGE AFTER OSSIAN.

' Roll on, streamy Dart, to thy ocean home, emblem of eternity;
tell thy tale of sorrow to the sighing winds. Sad is the sound
of grief, as the moaning of pines in the vale of Lartor. The gray
mist hangs heavily on Bellivor. The long, weeping moss droops
from the withered oak, like nodding plumes o'er a chieftain's
bier. "Is not our brother low? Is he not gone to his narrow
house? Did we not rise to the chase together? Pursued we
not the prowling otter among the winding streams of the forest;
from Cranmere-fount to the steps of Dartington-towers? The
stunted oaks of Whisht-man are bowed with grief; his horn is
idle and their echoes are silent for ever. The moon is pale
on the moor; her beam is still on that lofty rock; long are the
shadows of the tors; now it is dark all over; night is dreary,
silent, and dark; our brother is seen no longer; he is gone
for ever."

Note 13.   Page 47.

' In platter grand, as Cæsar's dish
Designed for one immortal fish.'

This fish, a turbot of gigantic size, was rendered immortal by the 4th Satire of Juvenal. No dish being found large enough to contain the monster, Domitian called the Roman Senate together to deliberate as to whether the fish should be divided or a platter large enough to contain it whole should be ordered from the potter's. The latter prevailed:

'testa alta paretur
Quæ tenui muro spatiosum colligat orbem.'

Note 14.   Page 69.

' Train him aright, and hope to see
True scion of your ancient tree.'

Whoever has wandered much in the counties of Devon or Cornwall must have been struck by the frequency with which his eye has fallen on the framed picture of a fine forest tree, in full verdure, with a mighty bole and endless ramifications arising from it in all directions. This, on close inspection, he has discovered to be the genealogical Buller tree, which represents the wonderful resuscitation of that honourable family from a single member of it, who, to all appearance had succumbed to the disease of small-pox, then so frequently fatal. John Francis Buller, at that time unmarried and the

last of a long line of distinguished ancestry, was literally 'laid
out' in his coffin at Morval, when his coachman entering the
chamber to take a last look at his master opened the win-
dow, and at once, as if by a miracle, the fresh air brought
new life, and the apparent corpse arose and recovered. This
gentleman, who very properly lies at the root of the present
wide-spreading tree, was afterwards married in 1716 to the
beautiful Rebecca Trelawny, a daughter of the famous Sir
John Trelawny, Bishop of Bristol, who in 1688 was sent to
the Tower by King James II. The clergyman engaged in
performing the marriage ceremony between the fair Rebecca
and Mr. Buller was so shocked at the distress exhibited by
the lady that he refused to proceed with the service; on which
the Bishop, her father, ordered him at once to do his duty,
or he would himself perform the ceremony. Accordingly, in
spite of a heart-rending scene, the clergyman obeyed orders
and the twain became man and wife. It is believed the gentleman's comeliness had been sadly disfigured by the small-pox,
which might account in some measure for the lady's repug-
nance to the union. There is a fine old picture at Morval
which represents Rebecca as the fairest of Eve's fair daugh-
ters; and a noble member of the Buller family has often
been heard to say jocosely, that, if any good looks were found
among the Bullers, they were attributable to their descent
from the fair Rebecca Trelawny. At the present time, a
single tree would be useless, it would require a forest to re-
present the different branches of the Buller race.

PART SECOND.

Note 15. Page 91.

' Where, ages back, the miner's hand
With hollow grips had scored the land.'

From various authors of antiquity it has been ascertained beyond a doubt that the Phœnicians were well acquainted with the British Isles at a very early period. Homer mentions tin, which could have come from nowhere but Britain ; and Herodotus affirms that the Greeks obtained their tin from these islands, ' The Abbé de Foutenu,' Mr. Vallencey says, ' has proved that the Phœnicians had an established trade with Britain before the Trojan War, 1,190 years before Christ, and that this commerce continued for many ages.'—*The Celtic Druids.*

Note 16. Page 99.

' And every farmer then might fear,
The devastation far and near.'

The writer has passed a great portion of his life in the mountains of Wales, where rabbits and game were scarce, but foxes plentiful ; and yet, during the lambing season, it was a very rare thing to lose a lamb of which no account could be given; and when it occurred, the ravens, and not the foxes, were considered to be the culprits. Foxes will doubtless carry a dead lamb to their young; but that is no reason for saying that such a lamb was killed by foxes. The habit of the animal, when he gets among a flock of geese or turkeys is to kill all he can catch ; and he buries what he cannot eat for future use. Thus a fox, that had once taken to the blood of lambs, would destroy them to such an extent in wild districts where they are unprotected, that the destruction would soon be measureless ; in fact, the fox would become a wolf in miniature.

The following letter, received on March 8, 1848, and here given *verbatim*, contains an imputation, but no proof against the foxes :—

'SIR JOHN RUSSEL,

'I am your humbl servant George Molton. I should think you If you please to come to bentwitching And Hunt these foxes for I have lost two Lambs one on Monday night 21st February and the other on Saturday night 4th March

'Your humbel Servant

'GEORGE MOLTON.'

A story is told of the late Mr. Templer, of Stover, who kept foxhounds, though I believe the story has an earlier origin, that a grasping tenant of his, on paying his annual rent, invariably claimed compensation for damage done by foxes. The first year he had lost a duck or two; then it came to a few geese ; then it increased to lambs, for which last, how-ever, Mr. Templer always paid with a protest. At length, the farmer made his appearance with a more ominous face than usual. 'Bad job this year, sir; worse than ever; they foxes have been at it again, sure enough.' 'Well, what's the matter now, Thomas?' 'Well, your honour, this time they have fairly carried away our young calf.'

Templer's forbearance could go no further; so, turning his back upon him, he told him to make haste home, or the foxes would carry away the cow as well; and never paid him another shilling for fox-damage. It should be added the above is an exception to the usual spirit of the Devonshire yeoman.

Note 17. Page 103.

' Like sceptics at the source of Nile.'

According to Sir Roderick Murchison, Captains Speke and Grant have at length set at rest the unsolved problem of ages as to the true source of the Nile.

Note 18. Page 103.

' The granite pile of Crockern tor.'

Polwhele conjectures Crockern tor to have been the site, in the British period, of the Supreme Court of Justice for the cantred of Tamara. But Mr. R. J. King says, 'There is not the slightest evidence for the very existence of such a cantred. Still it is not impossible that Crockern tor may have been a British place of council. Open-air courts were common to them, as well as to the Teutonic and Scandinavian races.' At a later date,

Mr. King says, 'the stannaries of Devon were divided into the
districts of Chagford, Ashburton, Tavistock, and Plympton; the
four towns to which tin was brought to be stamped with the
royal seal before it could be conveyed out of the county.
Twenty-four stannators were chosen by each of these districts,
whose duty it was to attend the courts at Crockern tor once in
every year.   The Lord Warden of the Stannaries was generally
one of the most important personages of the West, and acted for
both Devonshire and Cornwall.   Sir Walter Raleigh, whose an-
cestral residence, Fardel, is situated on the borders of Dartmoor,
was, during his first Court favour, and whilst the Duchy of
Cornwall was in the hands of Elizabeth, appointed Seneschal of
Cornwall and Lord Warden of the Stannaries: an office which he
continued to hold until the accession of James.   The first Earl
of Bath, son of Sir Bevil Grenville, is said to have attended the
parliament at Crockern as Lord Warden, with a retinue of three
hundred of the first gentlemen of the West.   A Sub-Warden is
appointed for each county.'   We are told by Carrington that 'in
the year 1512, Richard Strode, Esq., one of the Strodes of
Newnham Park, and member for the borough of Plympton
Earle, for his exertions in procuring an Act to prevent blocking
up harbours with stream-works, was prosecuted, or rather per-
secuted, by the tinners in their court, then holden at Crockern
tor, and heavily fined.   On his refusal to pay the same, he was
confined in the most horrible and loathsome dungeon of Lydford
Castle, and kept in irons on bread and water for more than three
weeks.   But the result of this tyrannous act was a considerable
improvement effected by parliament in some of the most im-

portant stannary privileges.' But the glory of Crockern tor
has long since departed; the Lord Warden's granite chair,
the benches on which the jurors sat, and the granite slab which
served the purpose of a table, have either been carried away, or
have become so dilapidated as scarcely to be distinguishable
from the rocks of which the tor itself is constructed. Still it is
well worth a visit; it stands to the north of Two Bridges, about
a mile and a half from that famed hostelry.

Note 19. Page 105.

' Of wonders seen at Wistman's wood.'

Strangers are often informed by moormen that at Wistman's
wood a hundred old oaks may be seen standing at least a hundred
yards high: the fact being, that a hundred oaks may be found
there which are at least three feet high apiece.

Note 20. Page 107.

' From Dunnabridge to old Grimspound.'

When the moor is driven for estrays, such cattle as do not belong to farmers possessing common rights are confined in Dunnabridge Pound, which is a place of ancient origin near Prince
Hall. Grimspound is a remarkable amphitheatre or oval
mound on Hamel Down, above the village of Widdecombe. It
covers a space of four acres, and appears to have been a
British settlement of very remote date. From the close proxi-
mity of the Vittifer mines, and the many stream-works by which

it is surrounded, Grimspound is conjectured to have been a place
of considerable importance, when the Britons carried on a brisk
trade in tin with the Greeks and the Phœnicians.

Note 21.   Page 107.

' Or stride away o'er bog and fell
To sound the depths of Claccy-well.'

' The depth of Claccy-well Pool,' Mr. Carrington says, ' has
been tried with the bell ropes of Walkhampton church, which
are between 80 and 90 fathoms long, and also by truss ropes,
which, before carts came into use, were employed in this part
of the country for fastening hay, &c., on pack horses, but
without finding bottom.   Great numbers of fish have been
placed in it at different times, but never seen afterwards.   The
pool appears to be subject to periodical falls and rises.   On
April 22, 1824, at half-past three in the afternoon, it was higher
by $2\frac{1}{2}$ feet than at the earlier part of the same day, and it was
12 feet higher than that in April, 1823.   There is a constant burst
of water from the side of the hill below it.   The soil around is
partly gravel and partly clay, affording traces either that it was
the crater of an extinct volcano, or the shaft of an ancient mine.
The circumference of the pool, at the edge of the water, is 305
yards, the perpendicular height of the bank on the back and two
sides 35 feet, and in the front about 6 feet, where it sometimes
overflows.'

PRINTED BY SPOTTISWOODE AND CO., NEW-STREET SQUARE, LONDON

GENERAL LIST OF WORKS

PUBLISHED BY

MESSRS. LONGMAN, GREEN, AND CO.

39 PATERNOSTER ROW, LONDON.

—◆—

THE CAPITAL OF THE TYCOON: A Narrative of a Three Years' Residence in Japan. By Sir RUTHERFORD ALCOCK, K.C.B., Her Majesty's Envoy Extraordinary and Minister Plenipotentiary in Japan. 2 vols. 8vo with Maps and above 100 Illustrations.

SIR JOHN ELIOT: a Biography. By JOHN FORSTER. With Two Portraits, from original Paintings at Port Eliot. [*Just ready.*]

HISTORY OF THE REFORMATION IN EUROPE IN THE TIME OF CALVIN. By J. H. MERLE D'AUBIGNÉ, D.D., President of the Theological School of Geneva, and Vice-President of the Société Evangélique; Author of *History of the Reformation of the Sixteenth Century.* VOLS. I. and II. 8vo

THE PENTATEUCH AND BOOK OF JOSHUA, Critically Examined. PART I. The Pentateuch Examined as an Historical Narrative. By the Right Rev. JOHN WILLIAM COLENSO, D.D., BISHOP of NATAL. Second Edition, revised. 8vo 6*s.* PART II. *The Age and Authorship of the Pentateuch Considered*, is nearly ready.

THE STORY OF A SIBERIAN EXILE. By M. RUFIN PIETROWSKI. Followed by a Narrative of Recent Events in Poland. Translated from the French. Post 8vo 7*s* 6*d*

REMINISCENCES OF THE LIFE AND CHARACTER OF COUNT CAVOUR. By WILLIAM DE LA RIVE. Translated from the French by EDWARD ROMILLY. 8vo 8*s* 6*d*

JEFFERSON AND THE AMERICAN DEMOCRACY: An Historical Study. By CORNELIS DE WITT. Translated, with the Author's permission, by R. S. H. CHURCH. 8vo 14*s*

DEMOCRACY IN AMERICA. By ALEXIS DE TOCQUEVILLE. Translated by HENRY REEVE, Esq. New Edition, with an Introductory Notice by the Translator. 2 vols. 8vo 21*s*

AUTOBIOGRAPHY OF THE EMPEROR CHARLES V. Recently Discovered in the Portuguese Language by Baron Kervyn de Lettenhove, Member of the Royal Academy of Belgium. Translated by LEONARD FRANCIS SIMPSON, M.R.S.L. Post 8vo 6*s* 6*d*

THE LAW OF NATIONS CONSIDERED AS INDEPENDENT POLITICAL COMMUNITIES. By TRAVERS TWISS, D.C.L., Regius Professor of Civil Law in the University of Oxford, and one of Her Majesty's Counsel. PART I. *The Right and Duties of Nations in Time of Peace.* 8vo 12s

Part II., *The Right and Duties of Nations in Time of War*, is in preparation.

THE CONSTITUTIONAL HISTORY OF ENGLAND, since the Accession of George III. 1760—1860. By THOMAS ERSKINE MAY, C.B. In Two Volumes. Vol. I. 8vo 15s Vol. II. just ready.

H.R.H. THE PRINCE CONSORT'S FARMS ; An Agricultural Memoir. By JOHN CHALMERS MORTEN. Dedicated, by permission, to H.M. the QUEEN. With 40 Illustrations on Wood, comprising Maps of Estates, Plans, Vignette Sketches, and Views in Perspective of Farm Buildings and Cottages. 4to 52s 6d

THE HISTORY OF ENGLAND, from the Accession of James II. By the Right Hon. LORD MACAULAY. Library Edition. 5 vols. 8vo £4

LORD MACAULAY'S HISTORY OF ENGLAND, from the Accession of James II. New Edition, revised and corrected, with Portrait and brief Memoir. 8 vols. post 8vo 48s

THE HISTORY OF FRANCE. (An entirely new Work, in Four Volumes.) By EYRE EVANS CROWE, Author of the 'History of France,' in the *Cabinet Cyclopædia.* 8vo VOL. I. 14s; VOL. II. 15s

⁎ The THIRD VOLUME is just ready.

A HISTORY OF THE ROMANS UNDER THE EMPIRE. By the Rev. CHARLES MERIVALE, B.D., late Fellow of St. John's College, Cambridge. 7 vols. 8vo with Maps, £5 6s

By the same Author.

THE FALL OF THE ROMAN REPUBLIC: A Short History of the Last Century of the Commonwealth. 12mo 7s 6d

A CRITICAL HISTORY OF THE LANGUAGE AND LITERA-TURE OF ANCIENT GREECE. By WILLIAM MURE, M.P., of Caldwell. 5 vols. 8vo £3 9s

THE HISTORY OF GREECE. By the Right Rev. the LORD BISHOP OF ST. DAVID'S (the Rev. Connop Thirlwall). 8 vols. 8vo with Maps, £3 ; an Edition in 8 vols. fcp 8vo 28s

HISTORICAL AND CHRONOLOGICAL ENCYCLOPÆDIA, presenting in a brief and convenient form Chronological Notices of all the Great Events of Universal History ; including Treaties, Alliances, Wars, Battles, &c. ; Incidents in the Lives of Great and Distinguished Men and their Works; Scientific and Geographical Discoveries; Mechanical Inventions, and Social, Domestic, and Economical Improvements. By B. B. WOODWARD, F.S.A., Librarian to the Queen. 8vo [*In the press.*

THE ANGLO-SAXON HOME: a History of the Domestic Institutions and Customs of England, from the Fifth to the Eleventh Century. By JOHN THRUPP. 8vo 12s

LIVES OF THE QUEENS OF ENGLAND. By AGNES STRICKLAND. Dedicated, by permission, to Her Majesty; embellished with Portraits of every Queen. 8 vols. post 8vo 60s

LIVES OF THE PRINCESSES OF ENGLAND. By Mrs. MARY ANNE EVERETT GREEN. With numerous Portraits, 6 vols. post 8vo 63s

LORD BACON'S WORKS. A New Edition, collected and edited by R. L. ELLIS, M.A.; J. SPEDDING, M.A.; and D. D. Heath, Esq. VOLS. I. to V., comprising the Division of *Philosophical Works.* 5 vols. 8vo £4 6s VOLS. VI. and VII., comprising the Division of *Literary and Professional Works.* 2 vols. 8vo £1 16s

THE LETTERS AND LIFE OF FRANCIS BACON, including all his Occasional Works and Writings not already printed among his *Philosophical, Literary,* or *Professional Works.* Collected and chronologically arranged, with a Commentary, biographical and historical, by J. SPEDDING, Trin. Coll. Cam. Vols. I. and II. 8vo 24s

MEMOIR OF THE LIFE OF SIR M. I. BRUNEL, Civil Engineer, &c. By RICHARD BEAMISH, F.R.S. *Second Edition*, revised; with a Portrait, and 16 Illustrations. 8vo 14s

LIFE OF ROBERT STEPHENSON, F.R.S., late President of the Institution of Civil Engineers. By JOHN CORDY JEAFFRESON, Barrister-at-Law; and WILLIAM POLE, Member of the Institution of Civil Engineers. With Portrait and Illustrations. 2 vols. 8vo *[In the press.*

THE LIFE OF SIR PHILIP SIDNEY. By the Rev. JULIUS LLOYD, M.A. Post 8vo 7s 6d

THE ROLL OF THE ROYAL COLLEGE OF PHYSICIANS OF LONDON; compiled from the Annals of the College, and from other Authentic Sources. By WILLIAM MUNK, M.D., Fellow of the College, &c. VOLS. I. and II. 8vo 12s each.

THE HISTORY OF MEDICINE: Comprising a Narrative of its Progress, from the Earliest Ages to the Present Time, and of the Delusions incidental to its advance from Empiricism to the dignity of a Science. By EDWARD MERYON, M.D., F.G.S., Fellow of the Royal College of Physicians, &c. VOL. I. 8vo 12s 6d

MATERIALS FOR A HISTORY OF OIL PAINTING. By Sir CHARLES L. EASTLAKE, R.A. 8vo 16s

BIOGRAPHICAL SKETCHES. By NASSAU W. SENIOR. Comprising Biographical Sketches connected with the French Revolution, Legal Biographical Sketches, and Miscellaneous Biographical Sketches. Post 8vo

HALF-HOUR LECTURES ON THE HISTORY AND PRACTICE of the FINE and ORNAMENTAL ARTS. By WILLIAM B. SCOTT, Head Master of the Government School of Design, Newcastle-on-Tyne. 16mo with 50 Woodcuts, 8s 6d

SAVONAROLA AND HIS TIMES. By PASQUALE VILLARI, Professor of History in the University of Pisa; accompanied by new Documents. Translated from the Italian by LEONARD HORNER, Esq., F.R.S., with the co-operation of the Author. 8vo   [Nearly ready.

THE LIFE OF WILLIAM WARBURTON, D.D., Lord Bishop of Gloucester from 1760 to 1779; with Remarks on his Works. By the Rev. JOHN SELBY WATSON, M.A , M.R.S.L. 8vo with Portrait, 18s

By the same Author.

LIFE OF RICHARD PORSON, M.A., Professor of Greek in the University of Cambridge from 1792 to 1808. With Portrait and 2 Fac-similes. 8vo 14s

BIOGRAPHIES OF DISTINGUISHED SCIENTIFIC MEN. By FRANÇOIS ARAGO. Translated by Admiral W. H. SMYTH, D.C.L., F.R.S., &c. ; the Rev. B. POWELL, M.A.; and R. GRANT, M.A., F.R.A.S. 8vo 18s

By the same Author.

METEOROLOGICAL ESSAYS. With an Introduction by Baron HUMBOLDT. Translated under the superintendence of Major-General E. SABINE, R.A., V.P.R.S. 8vo 18s

POPULAR ASTRONOMY. Translated and edited by Admiral W. H. SMYTH, D.C.L., F.R.S. ; and R. GRANT, M.A., F.R.A.S. With 25 Plates and 358 Woodcuts. 2 vols. 8vo £2 5s

TREATISE ON COMETS, from the above, price 5s

LIFE OF THE DUKE OF WELLINGTON, partly from the French of M. BRIALMONT; partly from Original Documents. By the Rev. G. R. GLEIG, M.A., Chaplain-General to H.M. Forces. *New Edition*, in One Volume, with PLANS, MAPS, and a PORTRAIT. 8vo 15s

MEMOIRS OF SIR HENRY HAVELOCK, Major-General, K.C.B. By JOHN CLARK MARSHMAN. With Portrait, Map, and 2 Plans. 8vo price 12s 6d

MEMOIRS OF ADMIRAL PARRY, THE ARCTIC NAVIGATOR. By his Son, the Rev. E. PARRY, M.A. Eighth Edition; with Portrait and coloured Chart. Fcp 8vo 5s

VICISSITUDES OF FAMILIES. By Sir BERNARD BURKE, Ulster King of Arms. FIRST, SECOND, and THIRD SERIES. 3 vols. crown 8vo price 12s 6d each

GREEK HISTORY FROM THEMISTOCLES TO ALEXANDER, in a Series of Lives from Plutarch. Revised and arranged by A. H. CLOUGH, sometime Fellow of Oriel College, Oxford. With 44 Woodcuts. Fcp 8vo 6s

TALES FROM GREEK MYTHOLOGY. By the Rev. G. W. Cox, M.A., late Scholar of Trinity College, Oxford. Square 16mo price 3s 6d

By the same Author.

TALES OF THE GODS AND HEROES. With 6 Landscape Illustrations from Drawings by the Author. Fcp 8vo 5s

THE TALE OF THE GREAT PERSIAN WAR, from the Histories of *Herodotus*. With 12 Woodcuts. Fcp 8vo 7s 6d

A DICTIONARY OF ROMAN AND GREEK ANTIQUITIES, with nearly 2,000 Wood Engravings, representing Objects from the Antique, illustrative of the Industrial Arts and Social Life of the Greeks and Romans. Being the Second Edition of the *Illustrated Companion to the Latin Dictionary and Greek Lexicon*. By ANTHONY RICH, Jun., B.A. Post 8vo 12s 6d

ANCIENT HISTORY OF EGYPT, ASSYRIA, AND BABYLONIA. By ELIZABETH M. SEWELL, Author of 'Amy Herbert,' &c. With Two Maps. Fcp 8vo 6s

By the same Author.

HISTORY OF THE EARLY CHURCH, from the First Preaching of the Gospel to the Council of Nicæa, A.D. 325. *Second Edition.* Fcp 8vo 4s 6d

MEMOIR OF THE REV. SYDNEY SMITH. By his Daughter, LADY HOLLAND. With a Selection from his Letters, edited by Mrs. AUSTIN. 2 vols. 8vo 28s

THOMAS MOORE'S MEMOIRS, JOURNAL, AND CORRESPONDENCE. People's Edition. With 8 Portraits and 2 Vignettes. Edited and abridged from the First Edition by the Right Hon. EARL RUSSELL. Square crown 8vo 12s 6d

SPEECHES OF THE RIGHT HON. LORD MACAULAY. Corrected by HIMSELF. *New Edition.* 8vo 12s

LORD MACAULAY'S SPEECHES ON PARLIAMENTARY REFORM IN 1831 AND 1832. Reprinted in the TRAVELLER'S LIBRARY. 16mo 1s

SOUTHEY'S LIFE OF WESLEY, AND RISE AND PROGRESS OF METHODISM. Fourth Edition, with Notes and Additions. Edited by the Rev. C. C. SOUTHEY, M.A. 2 vols. crown 8vo 12s

THE HISTORY OF WESLEYAN METHODISM. By GEORGE SMITH, F.A.S., Member of the Royal Asiatic Society, &c. 3 vols. crown 8vo 31s 6d

THE VOYAGE AND SHIPWRECK OF ST. PAUL: With Dissertations on the Life and Writings of St. Luke, and the Ships and Navigation of the Ancients. By JAMES SMITH, of Jordanhill, Esq., F.R.S. *Second Edition*; with Charts, &c. Crown 8vo 8s 6d

THE LIFE AND EPISTLES OF ST. PAUL. By the Rev. W. J.
CONYBEARE, M A., late Fellow of Trinity College, Cambridge; and the
Rev. J. S. HOWSON, D.D., Principal of the Collegiate Institution,
Liverpool. *People's Edition*, condensed; with 46 Illustrations and Maps.
2 vols. crown 8vo 12s

CONYBEARE AND HOWSON'S LIFE AND EPISTLES OF
ST. PAUL. The Intermediate Edition, thoroughly revised; with a Selection of Maps, Plates, and Wood Engravings. 2 vols. square crown 8vo
price 31s 6d

CONYBEARE AND HOWSON'S LIFE AND EPISTLES OF
ST. PAUL. The Library Edition, corrected and reprinted; with all the
Original Plates, Maps, Wood Engravings, and other Illustrations. 2 vols.
4to 48s

THE GENTILE AND THE JEW IN THE COURTS OF THE
TEMPLE OF CHRIST. An Introduction to the History of Christianity.
From the German of Professor DÖLLINGER, by the Rev. N. DARNELL,
M.A., late Fellow of New College, Oxford. 2 vols. 8vo 21s

PORT-ROYAL; A Contribution to the History of Religion and
Literature in France. By CHARLES BEARD, B.A. 2 vols. post 8vo
price 24s

HIPPOLYTUS AND HIS AGE; or, the Beginnings and Prospects
of Christianity. By C. C. J. BUNSEN, D.D., D.C.L., D. Ph. 2 vols.
8vo 30s

By the same Author.

OUTLINES OF THE PHILOSOPHY OF UNIVERSAL HISTORY,
applied to Language and Religion: Containing an Account of the
Alphabetical Conferences. 2 vols. 8vo 33s

ANALECTA ANTE-NICÆNA. 3 vols. 8vo 42s

EGYPT'S PLACE IN UNIVERSAL HISTORY: An Historical In-
vestigation, in Five Books. Translated from the German by C. H.
COTTRELL, M.A. With many Illustrations. 4 vols. 8vo £5 8s VOL.
V., completing the work, is in preparation.

A NEW LATIN-ENGLISH DICTIONARY. By the Rev. J. T.
WHITE, M.A., of Corpus Christi College, Oxford; and the Rev. J. E.
RIDDLE, M.A., of St. Edmund Hall, Oxford. Imperial 8vo 42s

A GREEK-ENGLISH LEXICON. Compiled by HENRY GEO.
LIDDELL, D.D., Dean of Christ Church; and ROBERT SCOTT, D.D.,
Master of Balliol. *Fifth Edition*, revised and augmented. Crown 4to
price 31s 6d

A LEXICON, GREEK AND ENGLISH, abridged from LIDDELL
and Scott's *Greek-English Lexicon*. Ninth Edition, revised and com-
pared throughout with the Original. Square 12mo 7s 6d

A NEW ENGLISH-GREEK LEXICON, containing all the Greek Words used by Writers of good authority. By CHARLES DUKE YONGE, B.A. *Second Edition,* thoroughly revised. 4to 21s

A DICTIONARY OF THE ENGLISH LANGUAGE. By R. G. LATHAM, M.A., M.D., F.R.S., late Fellow of King's College, Cambridge. Founded on that of Dr. SAMUEL JOHNSON, as edited by the Rev. H. T. TODD, M.A., with numerous Emendations and Additions. 2 vols. 4to in course of publication in Thirty Monthly Parts, price 5s each.

THESAURUS OF ENGLISH WORDS AND PHRASES, classified and arranged so as to facilitate the Expression of Ideas, and assist in Literary Composition. By P. M. ROGET, M.D., F.R.S., &c. *Twelfth Edition,* revised and improved. Crown 8vo 10s 6d

A PRACTICAL DICTIONARY OF THE FRENCH AND ENGLISH LANGUAGES. By LÉON CONTANSEAU, lately Professor of the French Language and Literature in the Royal Indian Military College, Addiscombe (now dissolved); and Examiner for Military Appointments. *Sixth Edition,* with Corrections. Post 8vo 10s 6d

By the same Author.

A POCKET DICTIONARY OF THE FRENCH AND ENGLISH LANGUAGES; being a careful abridgment of the above, preserving all the most useful features of the original work, condensed into a pocket volume for the convenience of Tourists, Travellers, and English Readers or Students to whom portability of size is a requisite. Square 18mo 5s

LECTURES ON THE SCIENCE OF LANGUAGE, delivered at the Royal Institution of Great Britain. By MAX MÜLLER, M.A., Fellow of All Souls College, Oxford. *Third Edition,* revised. 8vo 12s

THE STUDENT'S HANDBOOK OF COMPARATIVE GRAMMAR, applied to the Sanskrit, Zend, Greek, Latin, Gothic, Anglo-Saxon, and English Languages. By the Rev. THOMAS CLARK, M.A. Crown 8vo price 7s 6d

THE DEBATER: A Series of Complete Debates, Outlines of Debates, and Questions for Discussion; with ample References to the best Sources of Information. By F. ROWTON. Fcp 8vo 6s

THE ENGLISH LANGUAGE. By R. G. LATHAM, M.A., M.D., F.R.S., late Fellow of King's College, Cambridge. *Fifth Edition,* revised and enlarged. 8vo 18s

By the same Author.

HANDBOOK OF THE ENGLISH LANGUAGE, for the Use of Students of the Universities and Higher Classes of Schools. Fourth Edition. Crown 8vo 7s 6d

ELEMENTS OF COMPARATIVE PHILOLOGY. 8vo 21s

MANUAL OF ENGLISH LITERATURE, HISTORICAL AND CRITICAL; with a Chapter on English Metres. For the use of Schools and Colleges. By THOMAS ARNOLD, B.A., Professor of English Literature, Cath. Univ. Ireland. Post 8vo 10s 6d

ON TRANSLATING HOMER: Three Lectures given at Oxford. By MATTHEW ARNOLD, M.A., Professor of Poetry in the University of Oxford, and formerly Fellow of Oriel College. Crown 8vo 3s 6d—MR. ARNOLD's *Last Words on Translating Homer*, price 3s 6d

JERUSALEM: A Sketch of the City and Temple, from the Earliest Times to the Siege by Titus. By THOMAS LEWIN, M.A. With Map and Illustrations. 8vo 10s

PEAKS, PASSES, AND GLACIERS; a Series of Excursions by Members of the Alpine Club. Edited by J. BALL, M.R.I.A., F.L.S. Fourth Edition; with Maps, Illustrations, and Woodcuts. Square crown 8vo 21s—TRAVELLERS' EDITION, condensed, 16mo 5s 6d

SECOND SERIES OF PEAKS, PASSES, AND GLACIERS. Edited by E. S. KENNEDY, M.A., F.R.G.S., President of the Alpine Club. With 4 DOUBLE MAPS and 10 Single Maps by E. WELLER, F.R.G.S.; and 51 Illustrations on Wood by E. WHYMPER and G. PEARSON. 2 vols. square crown 8vo 42s

NINETEEN MAPS OF THE ALPINE DISTRICTS; from the First and Second Series of *Peaks, Passes, and Glaciers*. Square crown 8vo price 7s 6d

MOUNTAINEERING IN 1861; a Vacation Tour. By JOHN TYNDALL, F.R.S., Professor of Natural Philosophy in the Royal Institution of Great Britain. Square crown 8vo with 2 Views, 7s 6d

A SUMMER TOUR IN THE GRISONS AND ITALIAN VALLEYS OF THE BERNINA. By Mrs. HENRY FRESHFIELD. With 2 coloured Maps and 4 Views. Post 8vo 10s 6d

By the same Author.

ALPINE BYWAYS; or, Light Leaves gathered in 1859 and 1860. With 8 Illustrations and 4 Route Maps. Post 8vo 10s 6d

A LADY'S TOUR ROUND MONTE ROSA; including Visits to the Italian Valleys of Anzasca, Mastalone, Camasco, Sesia, Lys, Challant, Aosta, and Cogne. With Map and Illustrations. Post 8vo 14s

THE ALPS; or, Sketches of Life and Nature in the Mountains. By Baron H. VON BERLEPSCH. Translated by the Rev. LESLIE STEPHEN, M.A. With 17 Tinted Illustrations, 8vo 15s

THEBES, ITS TOMBS AND THEIR TENANTS, Ancient and Modern; including a Record of Excavations in the Necropolis. By A. HENRY RHIND, F.S.A. With 17 Illustrations, including a Map. Royal 8vo 18s

LETTERS FROM ITALY AND SWITZERLAND. By FELIX MENDELSSOHN-BARTHOLDY. Translated from the German by LADY WALLACE. *Second Edition*, revised. Post 8vo 9s 6d

A GUIDE TO THE PYRENEES; especially intended for the use of Mountaineers. By CHARLES PACKE. With Frontispiece and 3 Maps. Fcp 8vo 6s

The MAP of the *Central Pyrenees*, separately, price 3s 6d

HERZEGOVINA; or, Omer Pacha and the Christian Rebels: With a Brief Account of Servia, its Social, Political, and Financial Condition. By Lieut. G. ARBUTHNOT, R.H.A., F.R.G.S. Post 8vo, Frontispiece and Map, 10s 6d

CANADA AND THE CRIMEA; or, Sketches of a Soldier's Life, from the Journals and Correspondence of the late Major RANKEN, R.E. Edited by his Brother, W. B. RANKEN. *Second Edition.* Post 8vo, with Portrait, price 7s 6d

NOTES ON MEXICO IN 1861 AND 1862, Politically and Socially considered. By CHARLES LEMPRIERE, D.C.L., of the Inner Temple, and Law Fellow of St. John's College, Oxford. With Map and 10 Woodcuts. Post 8vo 12s 6d

EXPLORATIONS IN LABRADOR, the Country of the Montagnais and Nasquapee Indians. By HENRY YOULE HIND, M.A., F.R.G.S., Professor of Chemistry and Geology in the University of Trinity College, Toronto. 2 vols. [*Just ready.*

By the same Author.

NARRATIVE OF THE CANADIAN RED RIVER EXPLORING EXPEDITION OF 1857; and of the ASSINNIBOINE AND SASKATCHEWAN EXPLORING EXPEDITION OF 1858. With several Coloured Maps and Plans, numerous Woodcuts, and 20 Chromoxylographic Engravings. 2 vols. 8vo 42s

HAWAII; the Past, Present, and Future of its Island-kingdom: An Historical Account of the Sandwich Islands (Polynesia). By MANLEY HOPKINS, Hawaiian Consul-General. Post 8vo. Map and Illustrations, price 12s 6d

WILD LIFE ON THE FJELDS OF NORWAY. By FRANCIS M. WYNDHAM. With Maps and Woodcuts. Post 8vo 10s 6d

THE LAKE REGIONS OF CENTRAL AFRICA: A Picture of Exploration. By RICHARD F. BURTON, Captain H.M. Indian Army. 2 vols. 8vo, Map and Illustrations, 31s 6d

By the same Author.

FIRST FOOTSTEPS IN EAST AFRICA; or, An Exploration of Harar. With Maps and coloured Illustrations. 8vo 18s

PERSONAL NARRATIVE OF A PILGRIMAGE TO EL MEDINAH and MECCAH. *Second Edition*; with numerous Illustrations. 2 vols. crown 8vo 24s

THE CITY OF THE SAINTS; and Across the Rocky Mountains to California. *Second Edition*; with Maps and Illustrations. 8vo 18s

THE AFRICANS AT HOME: 'A Popular Description of Africa and the Africans, condensed from the Accounts of African Travellers from the time of Mungo Park to the Present Day. By the Rev. R. M. MacBrair, M.A. Fcp 8vo, Map and 70 Woodcuts, 7s 6d

LOWER BRITTANY AND THE BIBLE; its Priests and People: with Notes on Religious and Civil Liberty in France. By James Bromfield, Author of 'Brittany and the Bible,' &c. Post 8vo 9s

SOCIAL LIFE AND MANNERS IN AUSTRALIA; Being the Notes of Eight Years' Experience. By a Resident. Post 8vo 5s

IMPRESSIONS OF ROME, FLORENCE, AND TURIN. By the Author of *Amy Herbert*. Crown 8vo 7s 6d

AN AGRICULTURAL TOUR IN BELGIUM, HOLLAND, AND ON THE RHINE; With Practical Notes on the Peculiarities of Flemish Husbandry. By Robert Scott Burn. Post 8vo with 43 Woodcuts, 7s

A WEEK AT THE LAND'S END. By J. T. Blight; assisted by E. H. Rodd, R. Q. Couch, and J. Ralfs. With Map and 96 Woodcuts by the Author. Fcp 8vo 6s 6d

VISITS TO REMARKABLE PLACES: Old Halls, Battle-Fields, and Scenes illustrative of Striking Passages in English History and Poetry. By William Howitt. With about 80 Wood Engravings. 2 vols. square crown 8vo 25s

By the same Author.

THE RURAL LIFE OF ENGLAND. Cheaper Edition. With Woodcuts by Bewick and Williams. Medium 8vo 12s 6d

ESSAYS ON SCIENTIFIC AND OTHER SUBJECTS, contributed to the *Edinburgh* and *Quarterly Reviews*. By Sir Henry Holland, Bart., M.D., F.R.S., Physician-in-Ordinary to the Queen. *Second Edition.* 8vo 14s

By the same Author.

MEDICAL NOTES AND REFLECTIONS. *Third Edition*, revised, with some Additions. 8vo 18s

CHAPTERS ON MENTAL PHYSIOLOGY; founded chiefly on Chapters contained in *Medical Notes and Reflections. Second Edition.* Post 8vo 8s 6d

PSYCHOLOGICAL INQUIRIES: in a Series of Essays intended to illustrate the Influence of the Physical Organisation on the Mental Faculties. By Sir Benjamin C. Brodie, Bart., &c. Fcp 8vo 5s PART II. Essays intended to illustrate some Points in the Physical and Moral History of Man. Fcp 8vo 5s

AN INTRODUCTION TO MENTAL PHILOSOPHY, on the Inductive Method. By J. D. MORELL, M.A., LL.D. 8vo 12s

By the same Author.

ELEMENTS OF PSYCHOLOGY: Part I., containing the Analysis of the Intellectual Powers. Post 8vo 7s 6d

OUTLINE OF THE NECESSARY LAWS OF THOUGHT: A Treatise on Pure and Applied Logic. By the Most Rev. WILLIAM THOMSON, D.D., Lord Archbishop of York. *Fifth Edition.* Post 8vo 5s 6d

THE CYCLOPÆDIA OF ANATOMY AND PHYSIOLOGY. Edited by ROBERT B. TODD, M.D., F.R.S. Assisted in the various departments by nearly all the most eminent Cultivators of Physiological Science of the present age. 5 vols. 8vo with 2,853 Woodcuts, price £6 6s

A DICTIONARY OF PRACTICAL MEDICINE: Comprising General Pathology, the Nature and Treatment of Diseases, Morbid Structures, and the Disorders especially incidental to Climates, to Sex, and to the different Epochs of Life. By JAMES COPLAND, M.D., F.R.S. 3 vols. 8vo price £5 11s

HEAT CONSIDERED AS A MODE OF MOTION: A Course of Lectures delivered at the Royal Institution of Great Britain. By JOHN TYNDALL, F.R.S., Professor of Natural Philosophy in the Royal Institution. Crown 8vo with Illustrations. [*Just ready.*

THE COMPARATIVE ANATOMY AND PHYSIOLOGY OF THE VERTEBRATE ANIMALS. By RICHARD OWEN, F.R.S., D.C.L., Superintendent of the Natural History Department, British Museum, &c. With upwards of 1,200 Wood Engravings. 8vo [*Nearly ready.*

VAN DER HOEVEN'S HANDBOOK OF ZOOLOGY. Translated from the Second Dutch Edition. By the Rev. WILLIAM CLARK, M.D., F.R.S., &c. 2 vols. 8vo. with 24 Plates of Figures, price 60s cloth; or separately, VOL. I. *Invertebrata*, 30s; and Vol. II. *Vertebrata*, 30s

THE EARTH AND ITS MECHANISM; an Account of the various Proofs of the Rotation of the Earth; with a Description of the Instruments used in the Experimental Demonstrations; also the Theory of Foucault's Pendulum and Gyroscope. By HENRY WORMS, F.R.A.S., F.G.S. 8vo with 31 Woodcuts, price 10s 6d

VOLCANOS, the Character of their Phenomena; their Share in the Structure and Composition of the Surface of the Globe; and their Relation to its Internal Forces; including a Descriptive Catalogue of Volcanos and Volcanic Formations. By G. POULETT SCROPE, M.P., F.R.S., F.G.S. *Second Edition*, with Map and Illustrations. 8vo 15s

A MANUAL OF CHEMISTRY, Descriptive and Theoretical. By WILLIAM ODLING, M.B., F.R.S., Secretary to the Chemical Society, and Professor of Practical Chemistry in Guy's Hospital. Part 1. 8vo 9s

A DICTIONARY OF CHEMISTRY, founded on that of the late
Dr. URE. By HENRY WATTS, B.A., F.C.S., Editor of the *Quarterly
Journal of the Chemical Society.* To be published in Monthly Parts,
uniform with the New Edition of Dr. URE's *Dictionary of Arts, Manufactures, and Mines,* recently completed.

HANDBOOK OF CHEMICAL ANALYSIS, adapted to the Unitary
System of Notation. Based on the 4th Edition of Dr. H. Wills' *Anleitung
zur chemischen Analyse.* By F. T. CONINGTON, M.A., F.C.S.   Post 8vo
price 7s 6d

CONINGTON'S TABLES OF QUALITATIVE ANALYSIS, to accompany in use his Handbook of *Chemical Analysis.* Post 8vo 2s 6d

A HANDBOOK OF VOLUMETRICAL ANALYSIS. By ROBERT H.
SCOTT, M.A., T.C.D., Secretary of the Geological Society of Dublin.   Post
8vo 4s 6d

A TREATISE ON ELECTRICITY, in Theory and Practice. By
A. DE LA RIVE, Professor in the Academy of Geneva. Translated for
the Author by C. V. WALKER, F.R.S. With Illustrations.   3 vols. 8vo
price £3 13s

AN ESSAY ON CLASSIFICATION [The Mutual Relation of
Organised Beings]. By LOUIS AGASSIZ.   8vo 12s

A DICTIONARY OF SCIENCE, LITERATURE, AND ART: Comprising the History, Description, and Scientific Principles of every
Branch of Human Knowledge. Edited by W. T. BRANDE, F.R.S.L. and
E. The Fourth Edition, revised and corrected. 8vo   [*In the press.*

THE CORRELATION OF PHYSICAL FORCES. By W. R. GROVE,
Q.C., M.A., V.P.R.S., Corresponding Member of the Academies of Rome,
Turin, &c. *Fourth Edition.* 8vo 7s 6d

THE ELEMENTS OF PHYSICS. By C. F. PESCHEL, Principal of
the Royal Military College, Dresden. Translated from the German, with
Notes, by E. WEST. 3 vols. fcp 8vo 21s

PHILLIPS'S ELEMENTARY INTRODUCTION TO MINERALOGY.
A New Edition, with extensive Alterations and Additions by H. J.
BROOKE, F.R.S., F.G.S.; and W. H. MILLER, M.A., F.G.S.   With
numerous Woodcuts. Post 8vo 18s

A GLOSSARY OF MINERALOGY. By HENRY WILLIAM BRISTOW,
F.G.S., of the Geological Survey of Great Britain. With 486 Figures on
Wood. Crown 8vo 12s

ELEMENTS OF MATERIA MEDICA AND THERAPEUTICS. By
JONATHAN PEREIRA, M.D. F.R.S. *Third Edition,* enlarged and improved from the Author's Materials. By A. S. TAYLOR, M.D., and G. O.
REES, M.D. With numerous Woodcuts. VOL. 1. 8vo 28s; VOL. II.
PART II. 21s; VOL. II. PART II. 26s

OUTLINES OF ASTRONOMY. By Sir J. F. W. HERSCHEL, Bart., M.A. *Fifth Edition*, revised and corrected. With Plates and Woodcuts. 8vo 18s

By the same Author.

ESSAYS FROM THE EDINBURGH AND QUARTERLY REVIEWS, with Addresses and other Pieces. 8vo 18s

CELESTIAL OBJECTS FOR COMMON TELESCOPES. By the Rev. T. W. WEBB, M.A., F.R.A.S. With Woodcuts and Map of the Moon. 16mo 7s

A GUIDE TO GEOLOGY. By JOHN PHILLIPS, M.A., F.R.S., F.G.S., &c. Fourth Edition. With 4 Plates. Fcp 8vo 5s

THE LAW OF STORMS considered in connexion with the ordinary Movements of the Atmosphere. By H. W. DOVE, F.R.S., Member of the Academies of Moscow, Munich, St. Petersburg, &c. Second Edition, translated, with the Author's sanction, by R. H. SCOTT, M.A., Trin. Coll. Dublin. With Diagrams and Charts. 8vo 10s 6d

THE WEATHER-BOOK; A Manual of Practical Meteorology. By Rear-Admiral ROBERT FITZROY, R.N. With 16 Diagrams on Wood. 8vo 15s

ON THE STRENGTH OF MATERIALS; Containing various original and useful Formulae, specially applied to Tubular Bridges, Wrought-Iron and Cast-Iron Beams, &c. By THOMAS TATE, F.R.A.S. 8vo 5s 6d

MANUAL OF THE SUB-KINGDOM CŒLENTERATA. By J. REAY GREENE, B.A., M.R I.A. Being the SECOND of a New Series of MANUALS of the *Experimental and Natural Sciences*; edited by the Rev. J. A. GALBRAITH, M.A., and the Rev. S. HAUGHTON, M.A., F.R.S., Fellows of Trinity College, Dublin. With 39 Woodcuts. Fcp 8vo 5s

By the same Author and Editors.

MANUAL OF PROTOZOA; With a General Introduction on the Principles of Zoology, and 16 Woodcuts: Being the First Manual of the Series. Fcp 8vo 2s

THE SEA AND ITS LIVING WONDERS. By Dr. GEORGE HARTWIG. Translated by the Author from the Fourth German Edition; and embellished with numerous Illustrations from Original Designs. 8vo 18s

By the same Author.

THE TROPICAL WORLD: a Popular Scientific Account of the Natural History of the Animal and Vegetable Kingdoms in the Equatorial Regions. With 8 Chromoxylographs and 172 Woodcut Illustrations. 8vo 21s

FOREST CREATURES. By CHARLES BONER, Author of 'Chamois Hunting in the Mountains of Bavaria,' &c. With 18 Illustrations from Drawings by GUIDO HAMMER. Post 8vo 10s 6d

SKETCHES OF THE NATURAL HISTORY OF CEYLON: With Narratives and Anecdotes illustrative of the Habits and Instincts of the Mammalia, Birds, Reptiles, Fishes, Insects, &c., including a Monograph of the Elephant. By Sir J. EMERSON TENNENT, K.C.S., LL.D., &c. With 82 Illustrations on Wood. Post 8vo 12s 6d

By the same Author.

CEYLON; An Account of the Island, Physical, Historical, and Topographical; with Notices of its Natural History, Antiquities, and Productions. Fifth Edition; with Maps, Plans, and Charts, and 90 Wood Engravings. 2 vols. 8vo £2 10s

MARVELS AND MYSTERIES OF INSTINCT; or, Curiosities of Animal Life. By G. GARRATT. *Third Edition*, revised and enlarged. Fcp. 8vo 7s .

KIRBY AND SPENCE'S INTRODUCTION TO ENTOMOLOGY; or, Elements of the Natural History of Insects : Comprising an Account of Noxious and Useful Insects, of their Metamorphoses, Food, Stratagems, Habitations, Societies, Motions, Noises, Hybernation, Instinct, &c. *Seventh Edition.* Crown 8vo 5s

YOUATT'S WORK ON THE HORSE; Comprising also a Treatise on Draught. With numerous Woodcut Illustrations, chiefly from Designs by W. Harvey. New Edition, revised and enlarged by E. N. GABRIEL, M.R.C.S., C.V.S. 8vo 10s 6d

By the same Author.

THE DOG. A New Edition; with numerous Engravings, from Designs by W. Harvey. 8vo 6s

THE DOG IN HEALTH AND DISEASE: Comprising the Natural History, Zoological Classification, and Varieties of the Dog, as well as the various modes of Breaking and Using him. By STONEHENGE. With 70 Wood Engravings. Square crown 8vo 15s

By the same Author.

THE GREYHOUND: A Treatise on the Art of Breeding, Rearing, and Training Greyhounds for Public Running. With many Illustrations. Square crown 8vo 21s

THE ENCYCLOPÆDIA OF RURAL SPORTS; A Complete Account, Historical, Practical, and Descriptive, of Hunting, Shooting, Fishing, Racing, &c. By D. P. BLAINE. With above 600 Woodcut Illustrations, including 20 from Designs by JOHN LEECH. 8vo 42s

COL. HAWKER'S INSTRUCTIONS TO YOUNG SPORTSMEN in all that relates to Guns and Shooting. 11th Edition, revised by the Author's SON. With Portrait and Illustrations. Square crown 8vo 18s

THE DEAD SHOT, or Sportsman's Complete Guide; a Treatise on the Use of the Gun, with Lessons in the Art of Shooting Game of all kinds; Dog-breaking, Pigeon-shooting, &c. By MARKSMAN. *Third Edition*; with 6 Plates. Fcp 8vo 5s

THE FLY-FISHER'S ENTOMOLOGY. By ALFRED RONALDS. With coloured Representations of the Natural and Artificial Insect. *Sixth Edition*, revised by an experienced Fly-Fisher; with 20 new coloured Plates. 8vo 14s

THE CHASE OF THE WILD RED DEER in the Counties of Devon and Somerset. With an APPENDIX descriptive of Remarkable Runs and Incidents connected with the Chase, from the year 1780 to the year 1860. By C. P. COLLYNS, Esq. With a Map and numerous Illustrations. Square crown 8vo 16s

THE HORSE'S FOOT, AND HOW TO KEEP IT SOUND. *Eighth Edition*; with an Appendix on Shoeing and Hunters. 12 Plates and 12 Woodcuts. By W. MILES, Esq. Imperial 8vo 12s 6d

Two Casts or Models of Off Fore Feet—No. 1, *Shod for All Purposes*; No. 2, *Shod with Leather*, on Mr. Miles's plan—may be had, price 3s each.

By the same Author.

A PLAIN TREATISE ON HORSE-SHOEING. With Plates and Woodcuts. *New Edition*. Post 8vo 2s

HINTS ON ETIQUETTE AND THE USAGES OF SOCIETY; With a Glance at Bad Habits. New Edition, revised (with Additions). By a LADY of RANK. Fcp 8vo 2s 6d

SHORT WHIST; its Rise, Progress, and Laws: with Observations to make anyone a Whist-player. Containing also the Laws of Picquet, Cassino, Ecarté, Cribbage, Backgammon. By Major A. Fcp 8vo 3s

TALPA; or, the Chronicles of a Clay Farm: an Agricultural Fragment. By C. W. HOSKYNS, Esq. With 24 Woodcuts from Designs by G. CRUIKSHANK. 16mo 5s 6d

THE SAILING-BOAT: A Treatise on English and Foreign Boats, with Historical Descriptions; also Practical Directions for the Rigging, Sailing, and Management of Boats, and other Nautical Information. By H. C. FOLKARD, Author of *The Wildfowl*, &c. Third Edition, enlarged; with numerous Illustrations.   [*Just ready.*

ATHLETIC AND GYMNASTIC EXERCISES: Comprising 114 Exercises and Feats of Agility. With a Description of the requisite Apparatus, and 64 Woodcuts. By JOHN H. HOWARD. 16mo 7s 6d

THE LABORATORY OF CHEMICAL WONDERS: A Scientific Mélange for the Instruction and Entertainment of Young People. By G. W. S. PIESSE, Analytical Chemist. Crown 8vo 5s 6d

By the same Author.

CHEMICAL, NATURAL, AND PHYSICAL MAGIC, for the Instruction and Entertainment of Juveniles during the Holiday Vacation. With 30 Woodcuts and an Invisible Portrait. Fcp 8vo 3s 6d

THE ART OF PERFUMERY; being the History and Theory of Odours, and the Methods of Extracting the Aromas of Plants, &c. Third Edition; with numerous additional Recipes and Analyses, and 53 Woodcuts. Crown 8vo 10s 6d

THE CRICKET FIELD ; or, the History and the Science of the Game of Cricket. By the Rev. J. PYCROFT, B.A., Trin. Coll. Oxon. *Fourth Edition*; with 2 Plates. Fcp 8vo 5s

By the same Author.

THE CRICKET TUTOR ; a Treatise exclusively Practical, dedicated to the Captains of Elevens in Public Schools. 18mo 1s

THE WARDEN : a Novel. By ANTHONY TROLLOPE. New and cheaper Edition. Crown 8vo 3s 6d

By the same Author.

BARCHESTER TOWERS : A Sequel to the *Warden*. New and cheaper Edition. Crown 8vo 5s

ELLICE : A Tale. By L. N. COMYN. Post 8vo 9s 6d

THE LAST OF THE OLD SQUIRES : A Sketch. By the Rev. J. W. WARTER, B.D., Vicar of West Tarring, Sussex. *Second Edition.* Fcp. 8vo 4s 6d

THE ROMANCE OF A DULL LIFE. Second Edition, revised. Post 8vo 9s 6d

By the same Author.

MORNING CLOUDS. Second and cheaper Edition, revised throughout. Fcp 8vo 5s

THE AFTERNOON OF LIFE. Second and cheaper Edition, revised throughout. Fcp 8vo 5s

PROBLEMS IN HUMAN NATURE. Post 8vo 5s

THE TALES AND STORIES OF THE AUTHOR OF AMY HERBERT. New and cheaper Edition, in 10 vols. crown 8vo price £1 14s 6d boards ; or each work separately, complete in a single volume.

AMY HERBERT	2s 6d	IVORS	3s 6d
GERTRUDE	2s 6d	KATHERINE ASHTON	3s 6d
The EARL'S DAUGHTER	2s 6d	MARGARET PERCIVAL	5s 0d
EXPERIENCE of LIFE	2s 6d	LANETON PARSONAGE	4s 6d
CLEVE HALL	3s 6d	URSULA	4s 6d

*** Each work may be had separately in cloth, with gilt edges, at One Shilling per volume extra.

SUNSETS AND SUNSHINE; or, Varied Aspects of Life. By ERSKINE NEALE, M.A., Vicar of Exning, and Chaplain to the Earl of Huntingdon. Post 8vo 8s 6d

MY LIFE, AND WHAT SHALL I DO WITH IT? A Question for Young Gentlewomen. By an OLD MAID. *Fourth Edition.* Fcp 8vo 6s

DEACONESSES : An Essay on the Official Help of Women in Parochial Work and in Charitable Institutions. By the Rev. J. S. HOWSON, D.D., Principal of the Collegiate Institution, Liverpool. Fcp 8vo 5s

ESSAYS IN ECCLESIASTICAL BIOGRAPHY. By the Right Hon. Sir JAMES STEPHEN, LL.D. Fourth Edition, with a Biographical Notice of the Author, by his Son. 8vo 14s

By the same Author.

LECTURES ON THE HISTORY OF FRANCE. Third Edition. 2 vols. 8vo 24s

CRITICAL AND HISTORICAL ESSAYS contributed to The Edinburgh Review. By the Right Hon. Lord MACAULAY. Four Editions, as follows:—

1. A LIBRARY EDITION (the *Tenth*), 3 vols. 8vo 36s
2. Complete in ONE VOLUME, with Portrait and Vignette. Square crown 8vo 21s
3. Another NEW EDITION, in 3 vols. fcp 8vo 21s
4. The PEOPLE'S EDITION, in 2 vols. crown 8vo 8s

LORD MACAULAY'S MISCELLANEOUS WRITINGS: comprising his Contributions to *Knight's Quarterly Magazine*, Articles contributed to the Edinburgh Review not included in his *Critical and Historical Essays*, Biographies written for the *Encyclopædia Britannica*, Miscellaneous Poems and Inscriptions. 2 vols. 8vo with Portrait, 21s

THE REV. SYDNEY SMITH'S MISCELLANEOUS WORKS: Including his Contributions to the Edinburgh Review. Four Editions, viz.

1. A LIBRARY EDITION (the *Fourth*), in 3 vols. 8vo with Portrait, 36s
2. Complete in ONE VOLUME, with Portrait and Vignette. Square crown 8vo 21s
3. Another NEW EDITION, in 3 vols. fcp 8vo 21s
4. The PEOPLE'S EDITION, in 2 vols. crown 8vo 8s

By the same Author.

ELEMENTARY SKETCHES OF MORAL PHILOSOPHY, delivered at the Royal Institution. Fcp 8vo 7s

THE WIT AND WISDOM OF THE REV. SYDNEY SMITH: A Selection of the most memorable Passages in his Writings and Conversation. 16mo 7s 6d

ESSAYS SELECTED FROM CONTRIBUTIONS TO THE *Edinburgh Review.* By HENRY ROGERS. Second Edition. 3 vols. fcp 8vo 21s

By the same Author.

THE ECLIPSE OF FAITH; or, A Visit to a Religious Sceptic. *Tenth Edition.* Fcp 8vo 5s

DEFENCE OF THE ECLIPSE OF FAITH, by its Author: Being a Rejoinder to Professor Newman's *Reply.* Fcp 8vo 3s 6d

SELECTIONS FROM THE CORRESPONDENCE OF R. E. H. GREYSON, Esq. Edited by the Author of *The Eclipse of Faith.* Crown 8vo 7s 6d

ESSAYS AND REVIEWS. By the Rev. W. TEMPLE, D.D., Rev. R. WILLIAMS, B.D., Rev. B. POWELL, M.A., the Rev. H. B. WILSON, B.D., C. W. GOODWIN, M.A., Rev. M. PATTISON, B.D., and Rev. B. JOWETT, M.A. Fcp 8vo 5s

ESSAYS AND REVIEWS. *Ninth Edition*, in 8vo price 10s 6d

REVELATION AND SCIENCE, in respect to Bunsen's *Biblical Researches*, the Evidences of Christianity, and the Mosaic Cosmogony. With an Examination of certain Statements put forth by the remaining Authors of *Essays and Reviews*. By the Rev. B. W. SAVILE, M.A. 8vo price 10s 6d

THE HISTORY OF THE SUPERNATURAL IN ALL AGES AND NATIONS, IN ALL CHURCHES, CHRISTIAN AND PAGAN: Demonstrating a Universal Faith. By WILLIAM HOWITT, Author of *Colonisation and Christianity*. 2 vols. post 8vo   [*Nearly ready.*

THE MISSION AND EXTENSION OF THE CHURCH AT HOME, considered in Eight Lectures, preached before the University of Oxford in the year 1861, at the Lecture founded by the late Rev. J. Bampton, M.A. By J. SANDFORD, B.D., Archdeacon of Coventry. 8vo price 12s

PHYSICO-PROPHETICAL ESSAYS ON THE LOCALITY OF THE ETERNAL INHERITANCE: Its Nature and Character; the Resurrection Body; the Mutual Recognition of Glorified Saints. By the Rev. W. LISTER, F.G.S. Crown 8vo 6s 6d

BISHOP JEREMY TAYLOR'S ENTIRE WORKS: With Life by BISHOP HEBER. Revised and corrected by the Rev. C. P. EDEN, Fellow of Oriel College, Oxford. 10 vols. 8vo £5 5s

MOSHEIM'S ECCLESIASTICAL HISTORY. The Rev. Dr. MURDOCK's Literal Translation from the Latin, as edited, with Additional Notes, by HENRY SOAMES, M.A. *Third Revised Edition*, carefully re-edited and brought down to the Present Time by the Rev. WILLIAM STUBBS, M.A., Vicar of Navestock, and Librarian to the Archbishop of Canterbury. 3 vols. 8vo   [*In the press.*

PASSING THOUGHTS ON RELIGION. By the Author of *Amy Herbert*. New Edition. Fcp 8vo 5s

By the same Author.

SELF-EXAMINATION BEFORE CONFIRMATION: With Devotions and Directions for Confirmation-Day. 32mo 1s 6d

READINGS FOR A MONTH PREPARATORY TO CONFIRMA- TION; Compiled from the Works of Writers of the Early and of the English Church. Fcp 8vo 4s

READINGS FOR EVERY DAY IN LENT; Compiled from the Writings of BISHOP JEREMY TAYLOR. Fcp 8vo 5s

A COURSE OF ENGLISH READING, adapted to every taste and capacity; or, How and What to Read: With Literary Anecdotes. By the Rev. J. PYCROFT, B.A., Trin. Coll. Oxon. Fcp 8vo 5s

LEGENDS OF THE SAINTS AND MARTYRS, as represented in Christian Art. By Mrs. JAMESON. Third Edition, revised; with 17 Etchings and 180 Woodcuts. 2 vols. square crown 8vo 31s 6d

By the same Author.

LEGENDS OF THE MONASTIC ORDERS, as represented in Christian Art. New and improved Edition, being the Third; with many Etchings and Woodcuts. Square crown 8vo   [*Nearly ready.*

LEGENDS OF THE MADONNA, as represented in Christian Art. Second Edition, enlarged: with 27 Etchings and 165 Woodcuts. Square crown 8vo 28s

THE HISTORY OF OUR LORD AND OF HIS PRECURSOR JOHN THE BAPTIST; with the Personages and Typical Subjects of the Old Testament as represented in Christian Art. Square crown 8vo with many Etchings and Woodcuts   [*In the press.*

CATS' AND FARLIE'S BOOK OF EMBLEMS: Moral Emblems, with Aphorisms, Adages, and Proverbs of all Nations: Comprising 60 circular Vignettes, 60 Tail-pieces, and a Frontispiece composed from their works by J. LEIGHTON, F.S.A., and engraved on Wood. The Text translated and edited, with Additions, by R. PIGOT. Imperial 8vo 31s 6d

BUNYAN'S PILGRIM'S PROGRESS: With 126 Illustrations on Steel and Wood, from original Designs by C. Bennett; and a Preface by the Rev. C. KINGSLEY. Fcp 4to 21s

THEOLOGIA GERMANICA: Translated by SUSANNA WINKWORTH. With a Preface by the Rev. C. KINGSLEY; and a Letter by Baron BUNSEN. Fcp 8vo 5s

LYRA GERMANICA. Translated from the German by CATHERINE WINKWORTH FIRST SERIES, Hymns for the Sundays and Chief Festivals of the Christian Year. SECOND SERIES, the Christian Life. Fcp 8vo price 5s each series.

HYMNS FROM LYRA GERMANICA. 18mo 1s

LYRA GERMANICA. FIRST SERIES, as above, translated by C. WINKWORTH. With Illustrations from Original Designs by John Leighton, F.S.A., engraved on Wood under his superintendence. Fcp 4to 21s

THE CHORALE-BOOK FOR ENGLAND; A Complete Hymn-Book for Public and Private Worship, in accordance with the Services and Festivals of the Church of England: The *Hymns* from the *Lyra Germanica* and other Sources, translated from the German by C. WINKWORTH; the *Tunes*, from the Sacred Music of the Lutheran, Latin, and other Churches, for Four Voices, with Historical Notes, &c., compiled and edited by W. S. BENNETT, Professor of Music in the University of Cambridge, and by OTTO GOLDSCHMIDT. Fcp 4to price 10s 6d cloth, or 18s half-bound in morocco.

HYMNOLOGIA CHRISTIANA: Psalms and Hymns for the Christian Seasons. Selected and Contributed by Philhymnic Friends; and Edited by BENJAMIN HALL KENNEDY, D.D., Prebendary of Lichfield. Crown 8vo   [*Just ready.*

LYRA SACRA; Being a Collection of Hymns, Ancient and Modern Odes, and Fragments of Sacred Poetry; compiled and edited, with a Preface, by the Rev. B. W. SAVILE, M.A. Fcp 8vo 5s

LYRA DOMESTICA: Christian Songs for Domestic Edification. Translated from the *Psaltery and Harp* of C. J. P. SPITTA. By RICHARD MASSIE. Fcp 8vo 4s 6d

THE WIFE'S MANUAL; or, Prayers, Thoughts, and Songs on Several Occasions of a Matron's Life. By the Rev. W. CALVERT, M.A. Ornamented in the style of *Queen Elizabeth's Prayer Book*. Crown 8vo price 10s 6d

HORNE'S INTRODUCTION TO THE CRITICAL STUDY AND KNOWLEDGE OF THE HOLY SCRIPTURES. Eleventh Edition, revised throughout, and brought up to the existing state of Biblical Knowledge. Edited by the Rev. T. H. HORNE, B.D., the Author, the Rev. JOHN AYRE, M.A., and S. P. TREGELLES, LL.D.; or with the Second Volume, on the *Old Testament*, edited by S. DAVIDSON, D.D. and LL.D. With 4 Maps and 22 Woodcuts and Facsimiles. 4 vols. 8vo price £3 13s 6d

HORNE'S COMPENDIOUS INTRODUCTION TO THE STUDY OF THE BIBLE. *Tenth Edition*, carefully re-edited by the Rev. JOHN AYRE, M.A., of Gonville and Caius College, Cambridge. With 3 Maps and 6 Illustrations. Post 8vo 9s

THE TREASURY OF BIBLE KNOWLEDGE: Comprising a Summary of the Evidences of Christianity; the Principles of Biblical Criticism; the History, Chronology, and Geography of the Scriptures; an Account of the Formation of the Canon; separate Introductions to the several Books of the Bible, &c. By the Rev. JOHN AYRE, M.A. Fcp 8vo with Maps, Engravings on Steel, and numerous Woodcuts; uniform with *Maunder's Treasuries*.   [*Nearly ready.*

INSTRUCTIONS IN THE DOCTRINE AND PRACTICE OF CHRIS- TIANITY. Intended chiefly as an Introduction to Confirmation. By the Right Rev. G. E. L. COTTON, D.D., BISHOP of CALCUTTA. 18mo price 2s 6d

BOWDLER'S FAMILY SHAKSPEARE; in which nothing is *added* to the Original Text, but those words and expressions are *omitted* which cannot with propriety be read aloud. Cheaper Genuine Edition, complete in 1 vol. large type, with 36 Woodcut Illustrations, price 14s Or, with the same ILLUSTRATIONS, in 6 volumes for the pocket, price 5s each.

GOLDSMITH'S POETICAL WORKS. Edited by BOLTON CORNEY, Esq. Illustrated with numerous Wood Engravings, from Designs by Members of the Etching Club. Square crown 8vo 21s

MOORE'S IRISH MELODIES. With 161 Designs on Steel by DANIEL MACLISE, R.A., and the whole of the Text of the Songs engraved by BECKER. Super-royal 8vo 31s 6d

TENNIEL'S EDITION OF MOORE'S LALLA ROOKH. With 68 Woodcut Illustrations, from Original Drawings, and 5 Initial Pages of Persian Designs by T. Sulman, Jun. Fcp 4to 21s

MOORE'S POETICAL WORKS. People's Edition, complete in One Volume, large type, with Portrait after Phillips. Square crown 8vo price 12s 6d

POETICAL WORKS OF LETITIA ELIZABETH LANDON (L.E.L.) Comprising the *Improvisatrice*, the *Venetian Bracelet*, the *Golden Violet*, the *Troubadour*, and Poetical Remains. New Edition; with 2 Vignettes. 2 vols. 16mo 10s

LAYS OF ANCIENT ROME; with *Ivry* and the *Armada*. By the Right Hon. Lord MACAULAY. 16mo 4s 6d

LORD MACAULAY'S LAYS OF ANCIENT ROME. With Illustrations, Original and from the Antique, drawn on Wood by G. Scharf. Fcp 4to 21s

POEMS. By MATTHEW ARNOLD. FIRST SERIES, Third Edition. Fcp 8vo 5s 6d SECOND SERIES, 5s

By the same Author.

MEROPE : A Tragedy. With a Preface and an Historical Introduction. Fcp 8vo 5s

SOUTHEY'S POETICAL WORKS; with all the Author's last Introductions and Notes. *Library Edition*, with Portrait and Vignette. Medium 8vo 21s; in 10 vols. fcp 8vo with Portrait and 19 Vignettes, 35s

By the same Author.

THE DOCTOR, &c. Complete in One Volume. Edited by the Rev. J. W. WARTER, B.D. With Portrait, Vignette, Bust, and coloured Plate. Square crown 8vo 12s 6d

CALDERON'S THREE DRAMAS : *Love the Greatest Enchantment, The Sorceries of Sin*, and *The Devotion of the Cross*, attempted in English Asonante and other Imitative Verse, by D. F. MacCARTHY, M.R.I.A., with Notes, and the Spanish Text. Fcp 4to 15s

A SURVEY OF HUMAN PROGRESS TOWARDS HIGHER CIVILISATION: a Progress as little perceived by the multitude in any age, as is the growing of a tree by the children who sport under its shade. By NEIL ARNOTT, M.D., F.R.S., &c. 8vo price 6s 6d

COLONISATION AND COLONIES: Being a Series of Lectures delivered before the University of Oxford in 1839, '40, and '41. By HERMAN MERIVALE, M.A., Professor of Political Economy. Second Edition, with Notes and Additions. 8vo 18s

C. M. WILLICH'S POPULAR TABLES for Ascertaining the Value of Lifehold, Leasehold, and Church Property, Renewal Fines, &c.; the Public Funds; Annual Average Price and Interest on Consols from 1731 to 1861; Chemical, Geographical, Astronomical, Trigonometrical Tables, &c. &c. *Fifth Edition*, enlarged. Post 8vo 10s

THOMSON'S TABLES OF INTEREST, at Three, Four, Four and a-Half, and Five per Cent., from One Pound to Ten Thousand, and from 1 to 365 Days. 12mo 3s 6d

A DICTIONARY, PRACTICAL, THEORETICAL, AND HISTORICAL, of Commerce and Commercial Navigation. By J. R. M'CULLOCH, Esq. Illustrated with Maps and Plans. New Edition, containing much additional Information. 8vo 50s

By the same Author.

A DICTIONARY, GEOGRAPHICAL, STATISTICAL, AND HISTORI-CAL, of the various Countries, Places, and principal Natural Objects in the World. New Edition, revised; with 6 Maps. 2 vols. 8vo 63s

A MANUAL OF GEOGRAPHY, Physical, Industrial, and Political. By WILLIAM HUGHES, F R.G.S., &c., Professor of Geography in Queen's College, London. New and thoroughly revised Edition : with 6 coloured Maps. Fcp 8vo 7s 6d

Or, in Two Parts : PART I. Europe, 3s 6d; PART II. Asia, Africa, America, Australasia, and Polynesia, 4s

By the same Author.

THE GEOGRAPHY OF BRITISH HISTORY; a Geographical Description of the British Islands at successive Periods, from the Earliest Times to the Present Day; with a Sketch of the commencement of Colonisation on the part of the English Nation. With 6 full-coloured Maps. Fcp 8vo 8s 6d

A NEW BRITISH GAZETTEER; or, Topographical Dictionary of the British Islands and Narrow Seas: Comprising concise Descriptions of about 60,000 Places, Seats, Natural Features, and Objects of Note, founded on the best Authorities. By J. A. SHARP. 2 vols. 8vo £2 16s

A NEW DICTIONARY OF GEOGRAPHY, Descriptive, Physical, Statistical, and Historical : Forming a complete General Gazetteer of the World. By A. K. JOHNSTON, F.R.S.E., &c. *Second Edition*, revised. In One Volume of 1,360 pages, comprising about 50,000 Names of Places. 8vo 30s

AN ENCYCLOPÆDIA OF CIVIL ENGINEERING, Historical, Theoretical, and Practical. Illustrated by upwards of 3,000 Woodcuts. By E. CRESY, C.E. *Second Edition*, revised and extended. 8vo 42s

THE ENGINEER'S HANDBOOK; explaining the Principles which should guide the Young Engineer in the Construction of Machinery, with the necessary Rules, Proportions, and Tables. By C. S. LOWNDES, Engineer. Post 8vo 5s

USEFUL INFORMATION FOR ENGINEERS: Being a FIRST SERIES of Lectures delivered before the Working Engineers of Yorkshire and Lancashire. By W. FAIRBAIRN, LL.D., F.R.S., F.G.S.   With Plates and Woodcuts.   Crown 8vo 10s 6d

SECOND SERIES: Containing Experimental Researches on the Collapse of Boiler Flues and the Strength of Materials, and Lectures on subjects connected with Mechanical Engineering, &c.   With Plates and Woodcuts. Crown 8vo 10s 6d

By the same Author.

A TREATISE ON MILLS AND MILLWORK.   VOL. I. on the principles of Mechanism and on Prime Movers. With Plates and Woodcuts. 8vo 16s

AN ENCYCLOPÆDIA OF ARCHITECTURE, Historical, Theoretical, and Practical. By JOSEPH GWILT. With more than 1,000 Wood Engravings, from Designs by J. S. Gwilt. 8vo 42s

LOUDON'S ENCYCLOPÆDIA of Cottage, Farm, and Villa Architecture and Furniture. New Edition, edited by Mrs. LOUDON; with more than 2,000 Woodcuts. 8vo 63s

THE ELEMENTS OF MECHANISM, designed for Students of Applied Mechanics. By T. M. GOODEVE, M.A., Professor of Natural Philosophy in King's College, London.   With 206 Figures on Wood. Post 8vo 6s 6d

URE'S DICTIONARY OF ARTS, MANUFACTURES, AND MINES. Fifth Edition, re-written and enlarged; with nearly 2,000 Wood Engravings.   Edited by ROBERT HUNT, F.R.S., F.S.S., Keeper of Mining Records, &c., assisted by numerous gentlemen eminent in Science and connected with the Arts and Manufactures. 3 vols. 8vo £4

AN ENCYCLOPÆDIA OF DOMESTIC ECONOMY: Comprising such subjects as are most immediately connected with Housekeeping. By THOS. WEBSTER; assisted by Mrs. PARKES.   With nearly 1,000 Woodcuts. 8vo 31s 6d

MODERN COOKERY FOR PRIVATE FAMILIES, reduced to a System of Easy Practice in a Series of carefully-tested Receipts, in which the Principles of Baron Liebig and other eminent Writers have been as much as possible applied and explained. By ELIZA ACTON.   Newly revised and enlarged Edition; with 8 Plates, comprising 27 Figures, and 150 Woodcuts. Fcp 8vo 7s 6d

A PRACTICAL TREATISE ON BREWING, based on Chemical and Economical Principles: With Formulæ for Public Brewers, and Instructions for Private Families. By W. BLACK. 8vo price 10s 6d

ON FOOD AND ITS DIGESTION: Being an Introduction to Dietetics. By W. BRINTON, M.D., Physician to St. Thomas's Hospital, &c. With 48 Woodcuts. Post 8vo 12s

HINTS TO MOTHERS ON THE MANAGEMENT OF THEIR HEALTH DURING THE PERIOD OF PREGNANCY AND IN THE LYING-IN ROOM. By T. Bull, M.D. Fcp 8vo 5s

THE MATERNAL MANAGEMENT OF CHILDREN IN HEALTH AND DISEASE. Fcp 8vo 5s

LECTURES ON THE DISEASES OF INFANCY AND CHILDHOOD. By Charles West, M.D., &c. *Fourth Edition*, carefully revised throughout; with numerous additional Cases, and a copious Index. 8vo 14s

THE PATENTEE'S MANUAL: A Treatise on the Law and Practice of Letters Patent, especially intended for the use of Patentees and Inventors. By J. Johnson and J. H. Johnson, Esqrs. Post 8vo 7s 6d

THE PRACTICAL DRAUGHTSMAN'S BOOK OF INDUSTRIAL DESIGN. By W. Johnson, Assoc. Inst. C.E. *Second Edition*, enlarged; comprising 200 Pages of Letterpress, 210 Quarto Plates, and numerous Woodcuts. 4to 28s 6d

THE PRACTICAL MECHANIC'S JOURNAL: An Illustrated Record of Mechanical and Engineering Science, and Epitome of Patent Inventions. 4to price 1s monthly. Vols. I. to XV. price 14s each, in cloth.

THE PRACTICAL MECHANIC'S JOURNAL RECORD OF THE INTERNATIONAL EXHIBITION OF 1862. A full and elaborate Illustrated Account of the Exhibition, contributed by 42 Writers of eminence in the Departments of Science and Art. In One Volume, comprising 630 Pages of Letterpress, illustrated by 20 Plate Engravings and 900 Woodcuts. 4to price 28s 6d cloth.

COLLIERIES AND COLLIERS; A Handbook of the Law and leading Cases relating thereto. By J. C. Fowler, Barrister-at-Law; Stipendiary Magistrate for the District of Merthyr Tydfil and Aberdare. Fcp 8vo 6s

THE THEORY OF WAR ILLUSTRATED by numerous Examples from History. By Lieut.-Col. MacDougall, late Superintendent of the Staff College. *Third Edition*, with 10 Plans. Post 8vo price 10s 6d

PROJECTILE WEAPONS OF WAR AND EXPLOSIVE COM- POUNDS. By J. Scoffern, M.B. Lond. late Professor of Chemistry in the Aldersgate School of Medicine. *Fourth Edition*. Post 8vo with Woodcuts, 9s 6d

Supplement, containing New Resources of Warfare, price 2s

A MANUAL FOR NAVAL CADETS. By John M'Neil Boyd, late Captain R.N. Published with the Sanction and Approval of the Lords Commissioners of the Admiralty. Second Edition; with 240 Woodcuts, 2 coloured Plates of Signals, &c., and 11 coloured Plates of Flags. Post 8vo 12s 6d

PROJECTION AND CALCULATION OF THE SPHERE. For Young Sea Officers; being a complete Initiation into Nautical Astronomy. By S. M. SAXBY, R.N., Principal Instructor of Naval Engineers, H.M. Steam Reserve. With 77 Diagrams. Post 8vo 5s

By the same Author.

THE STUDY OF STEAM AND THE MARINE ENGINE. For Young Sea Officers in H.M. Navy, the Merchant Navy, &c.; being a complete Initiation into a knowledge of Principles and their Application to Practice. Post 8vo with 87 Diagrams, 5s 6d

A TREATISE ON THE STEAM ENGINE, in its various Applications to Mines, Mills, Steam Navigation, Railways, and Agriculture. With Theoretical Investigations respecting the Motive Power of Heat and the Proportions of Steam Engines; Tables of the Right Dimensions of every Part; and Practical Instructions for the Manufacture and Management of every species of Engine in actual use. By JOHN BOURNE, C.E. Fifth Edition; with 37 Plates and 546 Woodcuts (200 new in this Edition). 4to 42s

By the same Author.

A CATECHISM OF THE STEAM ENGINE. in its various Applications to Mines, Mills, Steam Navigation, Railways, and Agriculture; with Practical Instructions for the Manufacture and Management of Engines of every class. *New Edition,* with 80 Woodcuts. Fcp 8vo 6s

HANDBOOK OF FARM LABOUR : Comprising Labour Statistics ; Steam, Water, Wind ; Horse Power ; Hand Power ; Cost of Farm Operations; Monthly Calendar ; APPENDIX on Boarding Agricultural Labourers, &c.; and INDEX. By JOHN CHALMERS MORTON, Editor of the *Agricultural Gazette,* &c. 16mo 1s 6d

By the same Author.

HANDBOOK OF DAIRY HUSBANDRY : Comprising Dairy Statistics ; Food of the Cow ; Choice and Treatment of the Cow: Milk ; Butter ; Cheese ; General Management of a Dairy Farm ; Monthly Calendar of Daily Operations; APPENDIX of Statistics ; and INDEX. 16mo 1s 6d

CONVERSATIONS ON NATURAL PHILOSOPHY, in which the Elements of that Science are familiarly explained. By JANE MARCET. 13th *Edition*; with 34 Plates. Fcp 8vo 10s 6d

By the same Author.

CONVERSATIONS ON CHEMISTRY, in which the Elements of that Science are familiarly explained and illustrated. A thoroughly revised Edition. 2 vols. fcp 8vo 14s

CONVERSATIONS ON LAND AND WATER. Revised Edition, with a Coloured Map, showing the comparative Altitude of Mountains. Fcp 8vo 5s 6d

CONVERSATIONS ON POLITICAL ECONOMY. Fcp 8vo 7s 6d

BAYLDON'S ART OF VALUING RENTS AND TILLAGES, and Claims of Tenants upon Quitting Farms, at both Michaelmas and Lady-Day. *Seventh Edition,* enlarged. 8vo 10s 6d

AN ENCYCLOPÆDIA OF AGRICULTURE: Comprising the Theory and Practice of the Valuation, Transfer, Laying-out, Improvement, and Management of Landed Property, and of the Cultivation and Economy of the Animal and Vegetable Productions of Agriculture. By J. C. LOUDON. With 1,100 Woodcuts. 8vo 31s 6d

By the same Author.

AN ENCYCLOPÆDIA OF GARDENING: Comprising the Theory and Practice of Horticulture, Floriculture, Arboriculture, and Landscape Gardening. Corrected and improved by Mrs. LOUDON. With 1,000 Woodcuts. 8vo 31s 6d

AN ENCYCLOPÆDIA OF TREES AND SHRUBS: Containing the Hardy Trees and Shrubs of Great Britain, Native and Foreign, Scientifically and Popularly Described. With 2,000 Woodcuts. 8vo 50s

AN ENCYCLOPÆDIA OF PLANTS: Comprising the Specific Character, Description, Culture, History, Application in the Arts, and every other desirable Particular respecting all the Plants found in Great Britain. Corrected by Mrs. LOUDON. With upwards of 12,000 Woodcuts. 8vo £3 3s 6d

THE CABINET LAWYER: A Popular Digest of the Laws of England, Civil and Criminal: Comprising also a Dictionary of Law Terms, Maxims, Statutes, and much other useful Legal Information. 19th Edition, extended by the Author; with the Statutes and Legal Decisions to Michaelmas Term, 24 and 25 Victoria. Fcp 8vo 10s 6d

THE EXECUTOR'S GUIDE. By J. C. HUDSON. New and enlarged Edition, revised by the Author. Fcp 8vo 6s

By the same Author.

PLAIN DIRECTIONS FOR MAKING WILLS IN CONFORMITY WITH THE LAW. New Edition, corrected and revised by the Author. Fcp 8vo 2s 6d

THE BRITISH FLORA: Comprising the Phænogamous or Flowering Plants, and the Ferns. 8th Edition, with Additions and Corrections; and numerous Figures engraved on 12 Plates. By Sir W. J. HOOKER, K.H., &c.; and G. A. WALKER-ARNOTT, LL.D., F.L.S. 12mo 14s; with the Plates coloured, 21s

BRYOLOGIA BRITANNICA: Containing the Mosses of Great Britain and Ireland systematically arranged and described according to the method of Bruch and Schimper; with 61 illustrative Plates. By WILLIAM WILSON. 8vo 42s; or with the Plates coloured, price £4 4s

HISTORY OF THE BRITISH FRESH-WATER ALGÆ: Including Descriptions of the Desmideæ and Diatomaceæ. By A. H. HASSALL, M.D. With 100 Plates of Figures. 2 vols. 8vo £1 15s

By the same Author.

ADULTERATIONS DETECTED; or, Plain Instructions for the Discovery of Frauds in Food and Medicine. By ARTHUR HILL HASSALL, M.D. Lond., Analyst of The Lancet Sanitary Commission. With 225 Woodcuts. Crown 8vo 17s 6d

CORDON-TRAINING OF FRUIT TREES, Diagonal, Vertical, Spiral, Horizontal, adapted to the Orchard-House and Open-Air Culture. By Rev. T. COLLINGS BREHAUT. Fcp 8vo with Woodcuts, 3s 6d

THE THEORY AND PRACTICE OF HORTICULTURE; or, An Attempt to Explain the Principal Operations of Gardening upon Physiological Grounds. By J. LINDLEY, M.D., F.R.S., F.L.S. With 98 Woodcuts. 8vo 21s

By the same Author.

AN INTRODUCTION TO BOTANY. New Edition, revised and enlarged ; with 6 Plates and many Woodcuts. 2 vols. 8vo 24s

THE ROSE AMATEUR'S GUIDE: Containing ample Descriptions of all the fine leading Varieties of Roses, regularly classed in their respective Families ; their History and Mode of Culture. By THOMAS RIVERS. *Seventh Edition.* Fcp 8vo 4s

THE GARDENERS' ANNUAL FOR 1863. Edited by the Rev. S. REYNOLDS HOLE. With a coloured Frontispiece by JOHN LEECH. Fcp. 8vo 2s 6d

THE TREASURY OF NATURAL HISTORY; or, Popular Dictionary of Zoology: in which the Characteristics that distinguish the different Classes, Genera, and Species are combined with a variety of interesting information illustrative of the Habits, Instincts, and General Economy of the Animal Kingdom. By SAMUEL MAUNDER. With above 900 accurate Woodcuts. Fcp 8vo 10s

By the same Author.

THE SCIENTIFIC AND LITERARY TREASURY: A Popular Encyclopædia of Science and the Belles-Lettres ; including all branches of Science, and every subject connected with Literature and Art. Fcp 8vo 10s

THE TREASURY OF GEOGRAPHY, Physical, Historical, Descriptive, and Political; containing a succinct Account of every Country in the World. Completed by WILLIAM HUGHES, F.R.G.S. With 7 Maps and 16 Plates. Fcp 8vo 10s

THE HISTORICAL TREASURY: Comprising a General Introductory Outline of Universal History, Ancient and Modern, and a Series of Separate Histories of every principal Nation. Fcp 8vo 10s

THE BIOGRAPHICAL TREASURY: Consisting of Memoirs, Sketches, and Brief Notices of above 12,000 Eminent Persons of All Ages and Nations. *12th Edition.* Fcp 8vo 10s

THE TREASURY OF KNOWLEDGE AND LIBRARY OF REFERENCE: Comprising an English Dictionary and Grammar, a Universal Gazetteer, a Classical Dictionary, a Chronology, a Law Dictionary, a Synopsis of the Peerage, useful Tables, &c. Fcp 8vo 10s

Uniform with the above.

THE TREASURY OF BOTANY. By Dr. J. LINDLEY. [*In the press.*

THE TREASURY OF BIBLE KNOWLEDGE. By Rev. J. AYRE, M.A.   [*In the press.*

INDEX.

www.ingramcontent.com/pod-product-compliance
Lightning Source LLC
Chambersburg PA
CBHW031106020726
47495CB00007B/2065